Breaking Boundaries

ISBN-13: 978-1545597231
ISBN-10: 1545597235

Short stories, New Zealand, 1950-1970s, biographical

Breaking Boundaries

Margaret Hunter

Margaret Hunter

DEDICATION

In Te Aroha we are truly blessed to have a Community Hospital.

This is a place where loving care is given to the sick, the frail and, sadly, sometimes to those leaving this life.

Where all people are respected, comforted and valued.

Heartfelt thanks to all those who are part of making our Hospital a welcome home for all those in need of care.

Contents

ACKNOWLEDGEMENTS

My daughter Jennie Robertson has devoted the last thirty years tending to the needs of her 'Cantabria Home & Hospital' residents. I know how demanding this work can be, both physically and mentally and I appreciate this chance to say how much I admire her and all carers who give so much to those who need them.

Again, thank you to my editor Bev Robitai. Your work with a 'gentle' editing hand has been much appreciated.

To Rod who does my first edit and ensures I do not run out of printer ink and paper, thank you.

Finally, to all my family and friends who encouraged this second book, grateful thanks.

BEST OF FRIENDS

Ailsa sat in the café, waiting for her friend Jean, who usually arrived ahead of her.

She didn't want to choose her lunch or order her coffee as it would be rude to start lunch without Jean, but she did wish she would hurry up as she felt awkward sitting there without having bought anything, Oh good. She spotted Jean across the road, parcels in hand, hurrying down the street.

As is quite common for Te Aroha, there was a healthy bit of a breeze blowing even though the sun was shining. Jean came rushing in and spotting Ailsa, came over and plonked herself down at the table.

"Sorry I'm a bit late," she apologised. "It took longer than I expected to find the right card for Penny. She's fifty-three this year, hard to believe. Then I had to stop at the pharmacy to get my blood pressure pills, and coming past the butcher's couldn't resist his beef bolar roast special. Great in the crockpot, vegies and all, just set and forget, nice and easy and it'll last me at least three meals. How are you love, and how is Bob?"

As Jean stopped to catch her breath, Ailsa said, "I'm fine thanks and so is Bob, but I am glad you're here Jean, I'm getting really peckish. Shall we get ourselves some lunch now?" They rose in unison to make their choices from the cabinets.

They were regulars at this café, liking the selection of food and coffees, the pleasant owners and the reasonable

1

prices. The latter very important, when your main income was the 'Super'.

Ailsa and Jean had been friends since school days. Ailsa grew up in a farming family–dairy, like most of the Waikato district. Mangaiti was on the way to Paeroa, and as the locals would say, 'If you blinked you would miss it'. Many years ago this was the site of a train station, now there was only a hall and a welcome rest area for cyclists using the cycle trail.

Jean's dad had been a civil engineer working for the Council when it was Piako County Council. They lived within a ten minute walk from the town clock so Jean was a real 'townie'.

The school years went quickly, but the times they were to remember most were the giddy, giggling teenage years. When boys, who they had always thought of as crass creatures, ceased to be a focus of scorn and instead became rather interesting, and the source of never-ending discussions.

The girls developed into quite stunning young ladies, with their fathers keeping a protective eye on them, and their mothers lecturing them on the possibility of boys' unwanted intentions!

Ailsa and Jean were different in both nature and appearance. Ailsa the quieter of the two and Jean the chatter-box. Ailsa was petite with hair tending to auburn and skin that freckled. Her turquoise eyes would sparkle when she was excited about something, hinting at hidden emotions behind her seemingly placid manner. She loved the homely things, needlework, knitting and crochet, all crafts taught by her mother from an early age.

Ailsa confided in Jean her dream of one day having a shop of her own. She would specialise in all types of materials needed for needlework etc. and most importantly, dressmaking. She envisaged offering a dressmaking service to those who needed a special occasion frock or ensemble. Her mind ran riot with ideas.

Jean's appearance belied her true nature. Tall and slender yet with curves in all the right places, she kept her long russet brown hair tied back in a ponytail. Unusual deep grey eyes indicated a serious nature; though when laughter came they changed to a lighter hue.

Jean was a bookworm, curious by nature about everything and everyone. She never had any doubt as to her intended career, she would become a teacher. Preferably at a High School where she could indulge her love of languages – English, Latin and French. To teach classic poetry, Lord Byron, John Keats and Robert Burns and the writings of the masters such as Charles Dickens, Jane Austen, and Shakespeare.

Her college education finished, Jean went up to Auckland where for almost three years she lived in at the Teachers Training College.

Ailsa began her sewing business working from home and her workload grew. She saved hard to fulfil her dream of a shop in town. She already had the name of it in her mind, 'Beautiful Creations.'

Over the years the girls kept in close contact, writing each other long letters about parties and dances and the boys that they met, enjoying catching up when Jean came back at term breaks. Ailsa was always slightly envious with Jean having a much more exciting life than she did and this did make her feel guilty at times.

Jean's years of study flew by and soon she was home again. Fortune smiled on her when a vacancy for a teacher came up at the same college where she had gained her University Entrance – good old Te Aroha College.

Life was a joy. Local dances, the occasional movie and eventually, they each met *the* special young man to whom they gave their heart.

Now they were a foursome and with both of the boys having a car, trips further afield became the norm. Camping holidays along the coast of Thames, Te Puru being especially popular with both of their families. Picnics and cook-outs on the barbie made with bricks stacked in a U shape and a sheet of metal across the top. It worked a treat. Great times, never to be forgotten.

Eventually wedding bells rang out. Yes, they did ring the bells in those days.

Ailsa and Jean sat back replete from their lunch, smiling at the reminiscing they had been enjoying. Surely this wasn't a sign of old age? After all they were only in their mid-seventies, just a couple of youngsters, as they often laughingly reminded each other.

Ailsa leant towards Jean and very quietly said, "What do you think of old Bill Johnson's latest goings on?"

"Why, what's he been up to now?"

"He's having it off with Merle Helton."

Jean screwed up her face. "Ooh, I don't believe it. Even she wouldn't be that desperate, surely. I mean to say, what could she see in him? He always looks like he needs a good scrub, and everyone knows he's an old soak and has never done an honest day's work in his life. You know, he even ripped poor old Mrs Ganes off. He charged her three times what anyone else would've when he trimmed her hedges."

"Well, it is true Jean. He took Merle to the RSA last Saturday, bold as brass, and him having left his wife only a month or so ago. Mind you, she's better off without him I reckon and I was told it was Merle who paid for the drinks too, stupid woman. She should know he's only looking for free rent, and a bit of the other I expect, given his past track record." Ailsa reached into her handbag for her hankie and blew heartily, as if to rid herself of Bill Johnson and his nasty habits.

Looking at her watch Jean said, "Crikey, look at the time, I'd better get going. I promised to collect Jill Wilson at two o'clock and take her to the docs. Her hip is plaguing her again something awful. She should have had that hip replaced years ago, but it's the old story, you have to be nearly crippled before you get an operation. And now she can no longer drive, it doesn't make life easy for her. If you ask me, the health system needs a ruddy good shake-up."

"Thanks very much," the women chorused to the lady owner as they left the café. And saying their fond farewells, left to go their separate ways.

Life had dealt an early blow to Jean, when a work accident took her husband's life while he was still quite a young man. Jean brought up her two children alone and had never remarried. Never wanted another man after her darling Fred. Later on with the support of family and friends, she went back to teaching. Her dearest friend Ailsa always there when needed.

Ailsa and her husband Bob had four children in quick succession. Quite apart from being a wife and mother, she also helped Bob with the milking and cared for the calves, never having a moment to spare. All thoughts of a shop of her own were for now, well and truly shelved.

Eventually, with family grown and left home, her dream came true. She had a stunning shop in town with all the supplies for handcrafts that anyone would want. Ailsa had never forgotten the first time she served a man. She had presumed he was shopping for his wife but no, he was the knitter, and as time went on Ailsa was to find quite a few men made handcrafts.

With her pleasant nature and helpful attitude, Ailsa's shop proved extremely popular and the business flourished.

Jean's teaching continued to give her immense satisfaction. Seeing generations of young minds expand and grow as the teenagers reached maturity was always rewarding.

Jean had retired from teaching at sixty-five, and then Ailsa and Bob sold the farm and moved into town. Bob had insisted on enough space for a decent sized vegie garden, and Ailsa looked forward to creating new rose gardens.

One of the highlights of the year in Te Aroha was the A.P & H show. Agriculture, Pastoral and Horticulture to be exact. This being held in the spring.

Ailsa entered the produce section each year and sometimes won with her broad beans, spinach or leeks. But she loved baking, and each year entered the chocolate cake section.

Jean's only interest was the baking and each year she entered her chocolate cake. She sometimes wondered why she bothered as year after year the winner was her best friend, Ailsa. But Jean never gave up hoping that maybe, one day…

Early one evening, Ailsa read an advertisement in the Piako Post, promoting the next A.P & H show to be held the following month, November. She pondered on how winning the chocolate cake competition was no longer enjoyable and then realised why.

Turning to Bob she voiced her thoughts. "You know Bob, I don't get a kick out of winning the cake competition anymore and I've just realised why".

"Okay, put me out of my misery love," Bob answered. "Why?"

"It's because of Jean. I always feel guilty because she never wins, and I nearly always do and I have so much compared to Jean. Her kids are both overseas and ours are still around. Then I have you, and she has no-one special at all."

Bob came across to Ailsa and cuddled her tight. "You really are a sweetie at times old girl." They stood like that for a couple of minutes until Bob said, "Jean does have someone you know, she has you, a very special friend. Now, are we ever going to have a meal tonight?"

And laughing, Ailsa went into the kitchen to start preparing dinner.

The morning of the A.P & H show arrived and Ailsa began to prepare for baking the cake. Everything was organised with almost military precision. Ingredients were put on the bench, along with her favourite mixing bowls and utensils lined up at the ready. With the oven turned on to heat up to the exact temperature, Ailsa was ready to start. First, prepare the cake tin.

It was as she mixed the dry ingredients that the accident happened. The sun was pouring in the window, nearly blinding her, and Ailsa quickly dropped the venetian blind. She'd forgotten to remove the salt pig that sat on the windowsill, and the wooden spoon full of salt flipped out, landing right in the bowl of dry cake mixture.

'Damn and blast,' Ailsa muttered, and stood hands on hip staring at the ruined mix. She would have to start all over again.

And then like divine intervention, the answer came to her. She grinned like a Cheshire cat and patting down her pinny took a deep breath as she continued on with her baking.

The old hall hummed with activity and chit-chat as the baking entries were set-up. Jean and Ailsa stood back and looked at their chocolate cakes.

Covered in slick shiny chocolate icing, the cakes looked perfect. But then they both knew that 'the proof would be in the pudding' or in this case – in the cake.

"Well, that's done," said Jean. "I don't know about you, but I would love a cuppa and a bite to eat," and the two friends wandered off in the direction of the refreshment tent.

It was a grand morning to be out and about. On this beautiful clear day Mount Te Aroha stood proud above the town, a magnificent benevolent backdrop. It was family time at Boyd Park with something for everyone. Children proud of their entries in the animal competitions, riders as immaculate as their horses competing in the dressage, wood chopping, always a popular event, tractor rides and of course gumboot-throwing amongst many fun events. Tents offered numerous wares, raffles, produce and a great assortment of food. The place hummed with happy people.

It was judging time for the baking entries. Back in the shed, Jean had been pointing out to Ailsa the fact that there were a couple of men putting in entries this year. Times are sure changing they agreed, and why not?

Jean smiled at Ailsa and asked, "Ready for another 1st, love?"

They watched as the cakes were checked one by one. Appearance first. Then cut, the slice checked for texture and moisture. Aroma – very important, and finally the tasting. The entrants held their breath. Time for the truth.

As Ailsa told Bob later, she wished she'd had a camera to record the astonishment, the open-mouthed amazement that Jean showed when the results were announced. For Jean had won first prize. For the rest of the day she couldn't stop smiling and Ailsa was so happy for her very best friend.

Bob was sympathetic to Ailsa when he learned she had missed out on winning with her cake. He commented, "At least you don't have to feel guilty this time."

Ailsa looked up at him. "You're quite right love, I don't feel guilty at all and really, I won too. Jean has had a wonderful day, and so have I."

Ailsa wandered into the kitchen and put the jug on for coffee. Her eyes were drawn to the innocuous salt-pig. She smiled to herself. So much for old wives' tales. Spilling salt isn't always bad luck, is it?

MISLEADING

The group of young people trickled slowly back onto the college grounds, sweaty and breathing hard from the long run.

Further back a striking tall young woman, her dark hair plastered damply to her forehead, suffered the attention of a band of lads. They laughingly gave her a hard time in a cocky macho manner.

"Come on Miss Larsen, admit it, you should have been leading us, not bringing up the rear," stated a lanky fair headed boy.

"Leave her alone Paul," came a feminine voice from the rear. "She wasn't on her own back there. There were quite a few of us who trailed the field, and not just girls either."

Miss Larsen just grinned. "Wait until I get in some running practice Paul. Then I'll give you a run for your money – no pun intended."

The group split, each to get cleaned up before they got ready to go home. Not before time as the siren screamed out the end to the school day.

Jan Larsen had a quick wash in the staff ablution area and returned to the staffroom. She checked out her schedule for Monday and began to pack her weekend work into her oversized satchel.

"Hey Jan, are you coming with us for a couple of drinks tonight? We thought we'd try out the Staffordshire Inn for a change."

Jan turned to look at Kate, a curvy blonde young woman that Jan thought looked more like a Playboy centrepiece than a teacher. "Not for me thanks Kate, I have heaps to do when I get home."

It was as well that Jan couldn't hear the chat that went on after she left. The general consensus being that Jan was a bit up herself, never wanting to mix with staff outside school hours. But they had to admit she was a good teacher, they all agreed on that.

Merging her nippy bright green VW into the dense Auckland traffic, Jan couldn't wait to get home. There she would sit back and share a wine or two with her partner. Lovely. Then Sam would help her prepare dinner. A much better option than drinking with work-mates in pubs!

The weekend flew by and another school week began. Jan was a bit worried when asked by the headmaster, Will Mason, to come to his office, but he soon put her mind at rest.

"There's nothing wrong Jan; it's just that we're about to have a new pupil start with us. Mark Watson is fourteen and he comes from a difficult background. His mother left the family a while back, shot through to Oz apparently and she's not expected back. The father moved down here from Whangarei thinking a change would help them all. The oldest boy managed to transfer his builder's apprenticeship to an Auckland company and he's fine, but the father said he's having a helluva job with Mark; sheer rebellion he reckons. Mixing with a bad crowd, sneaking out at night and he's sure the boy's drinking. He hopes he's wrong, but thinks Mark may be smoking dope, and says he's reluctant to start school - any school. I'd like to know why. It could be the feminine touch is what he's missing, that's why I want him in your class Jan. Anyway, let me know how you get on. Oh, and here's the report from his old school, this might be of help."

The following Wednesday morning the Head brought Mark to Jan's classroom. The boy was dark haired and solidly built, already shaving by the look of it. He looked more like sixteen than fourteen. His dark brooding eyes shot across at Jan and he held his chin up defiantly.

Jan welcomed him and introduced him to his classmates. She asked him to choose a seat and continued with the discussion on the threat to the environment from 'Climate Change'. It was noticeable that the newcomer took no part in answering or asking questions. All right, Jan thought. Early days yet.

When the bell sounded for lunch break, she asked Mark to stay back a few minutes. Trying to draw the boy out she asked, "What are your special interests Mark"?

The reply was instant. "None."

"Well then, what school subjects do you like best?" The boy repeated the first answer.

Jan took a deep breath. "In that case we will just have to evaluate your progress as we go along. Thank you Mark, you may go now."

In the staffroom Jan re-read through Mark's report and covering letter from his past school. Some things didn't add up. He had been keen on athletics – but was not the team type. In the classroom it seemed he had a keen enquiring mind, but the results weren't there. He was clever with his hands, in particular metalwork. But look at the low grades in all his written mathematical tests as well as history, science, biology and in particular, English. Give it time, Jan mused, and got on with her lunch.

It wasn't until phys'ed at two o'clock that Jan met up with Mark again. This was to be a revelation.

The shot-put area had three keen lads lining up and then Mark arrived and joined the line. The recent New Zealand wins at the Olympics had, Jan thought, created more interest in this sport. Over the next half hour Jack Bates, the phys'ed trainer, put them through the basics. Stance, balance and movement on the pad – even before he handed them the heavy metal ball. Jan noticed the determined look on Mark's face as he hoisted the ball for the first time. The session ended with push-ups and here Mark excelled. The 'well done' from Jack Bates drew no obvious reaction from Mark, but to Jan he seemed to stand a little taller after Jack's comment.

During dinner that evening, Jan talked to her partner Sam about her concerns for the boy. "A real closed shop he is," she said. "He gives out nothing, and yet I get the feeling he is deeply unhappy."

"Well, wouldn't you be if your mother had left you to go to another country?" Sam asked.

"I can understand that, but this is something more. Almost as if he is worried or frightened for some reason. Oh well, tomorrow I'll have a chat with his maths and history teachers, see how he is with them."

On that note they started to clear the table. TV next for a while, and a reasonably early night.

It was Friday before Jan got to speak with Mark's maths and history teachers. At the end of school they all stayed back for a while, and Jan was most appreciative. As they compared their findings a common theme appeared. After open discussions, it appeared Mark showed an excellent retention of facts. Amazing really as he didn't seem to refer to his textbooks at all. Homework was often not done and his writing – printing actually, was very poor.

Jan made a time to see the Head and took her concerns to him. "I may be wrong Will, but I think Mark has a reading problem which leads to writing difficulties. It's possible he's kept this hidden for a long time. If this is the case it would be a constant worry for him. Can you imagine how he must feel; that is if I'm right?"

Will leaned back in his chair and rubbed his chin. Jan smiled inwardly. Always a dead give-away that he was deep in thought. "Do you have any ideas on the best way to handle this?" he asked. "Or do you want me to have a talk with him?"

"Thanks for the offer Will, but no, not at this stage. I'll work on gaining his confidence for a while and perhaps then, offer him some after school tuition in my areas and see his reaction to that."

"Fine Jan, I'll leave it with you for now, thanks for keeping me informed."

It was the following week before the right time arose for Jan to talk to Mark. Knowing the lad's keen interest in environmental issues, Jan decided to ask his help with a project she had planned. Sneaky perhaps, but it could, and she hoped it would, work out for the best.

Mark's reaction was rather offhand. She saw a mix of pride in being asked to help, but there it was again – doubt, fear even? He did however agree, and they decided he would stay back Mondays, Wednesdays and Fridays to work on the project.

Mark's creativity came to the fore with his detailed drawings. Soil, mountain ranges, sediments, forests, volcanoes and oceanic life, were all beautifully done. Jan's praise of Mark was genuine and for the first time she saw him smile. She noticed however, that descriptive phrases were not done at school, rather as homework it seemed, and they lacked clarity. Jan would wait until the time was right and discuss this with Mark.

In the meantime he appeared to grow in confidence. His other teachers commented on his more cooperative manner and, Jack Bates reckoned that in Mark; the school had a future shot-put champion.

Jan remained a little aloof from the rest of the staff when it came to socialising. She had her own private life to lead and preferred to leave it that way. She did not however, begrudge Mark the time she stayed back to work with him. It never occurred to Jan that some people could make something of her helping the boy. Had she known the staffroom gossip she would have been horrified.

Jan got on very well with the Head, finding him a decent and fair man, and a good listener. She told him, "I think the time is right for me to have a straight talk with Mark. I'm beginning to wonder if he could even be dyslexic. If that is the case would we be able to get specialised help for him?"

"This has happened before Jan, though at another school where I taught, and yes, there is help available. I would help Mark in any way I could. See how you get on."

Finally the day came when after a good discussion on their progress with the project, Jan asked the question. "Do you have problems reading Mark? Do you sometimes have problems recognising words?"

Mark's face flushed and his head drooped.

"Please Mark, I really need to know. If that is the case, then I can help."

The lad looked up at her and tears welled. Looking embarrassed, he knuckled them away. "I can't read properly no matter how hard I try, even though I want to. Dad tells me what the text-books say and I copy what to write, but it's not easy. But I've not been cheating, honest Miss. The answers are mine."

Jan wanted to reach out to the lad, but kept her hands in her lap. They talked some more, and now the floodgates were open Mark poured out his worries and feelings, about school and home. Missing his mother and maybe letting his dad down too, was a heavy load for a young lad to carry.

Mark agreed to a meeting with the Head and this resulted in a planned visit to a specialist teacher who handled learning difficulties, including dyslexia. It would be up to her to decide the best way forward for Mark. Of course this was not to be divulged to other staff, there was to be no chance of Mark being caused embarrassment.

In the meantime, Jan and Mark continued the extra tutorials. If she had known the result these extra hours of teaching caused she would have been mortified.

Unpleasant staff gossip eventually reached the ears of the headmaster. Will Mason was a very worried man and immediately asked Jan to his office. "Please shut the door." he said. That, and his serious face, gave Jan concern.

"There is no other way to say this Jan. I'm sorry to have to tell you that there are rumours, rather unpalatable ones, going about. They are regarding you and young Mark Watson. I have no doubt that these rumours are untrue, but I have to ask you anyway. Are you involved in a physical relationship with the boy?"

Jan felt sick. She looked directly at the Head. "I think that is the most disgusting question I have ever had to answer," she said in a very quiet voice. "Of course the answer is no. You are fully aware of the work I am doing with Mark and the progress we are making. For God's sake, he is just a boy. A boy." Jan began to laugh and laugh.

Will Mason looked at her in astonishment. Of all the reactions he may have expected, hysterical laughter wasn't one of them. "I suspect I know who started these rumours and I'll talk to that person," he told her. "Jealousy can create bitter enemies. However Jan, I have to put the safety of my pupils first. I can see nothing humorous in this situation; how can you?"

Regaining her composure Jan said, "Perhaps if I explain. But first, I must be sure that this remains confidential, as it also involves another person."

Will Mason nodded his agreement.

Jan began. "I have, for the past three years, lived in a relationship with a wonderful partner. We mean the world to each other, and have accepted that we are outside what some people see as the 'norm.' You see, Sam's full name is Samantha. She and I are lesbians. We have no problems with this and have a close circle of understanding friends. But we choose to keep our personal lives separate from our work lives. Sam is a talented artist, a kind and caring person. I can assure you that I think Mark is a very nice lad, but to put it bluntly; I feel no physical attraction to any of the male sex, let alone Mark. At this time I have nothing further to say, and need time to absorb all you have told me," and Jan swiftly left the room.

That evening it was a sometimes heated discussion that Jan had with Samantha. Sam said she shouldn't have to put up with snide remarks and innuendos from anyone, especially at her work. Jan in tears shouted that she no longer wanted to teach there. In fact, she was no longer sure she even wanted to teach!

Sam reminded Jan of the brilliant work offer she had received and turned down because Jan didn't want to move to Wellington. Could this be the answer, a new start for them both?

There was one thing Jan knew for sure. Her love for Sam came first, and Sam felt the same. Whether right or wrong they made a decision, Sam would accept the work offer and they would leave Auckland.

Jan's resignation was sadly accepted by Will Mason. There was no leaving party at the school for her. The rest of the staff were not surprised, she'd never mixed with them anyway. They were told she and her partner were leaving Auckland for Wellington. A new job for her partner apparently.

With the specialist help Mark received, his schoolwork improved in leaps and bounds. He always remembered that super teacher he had to thank for this. Gee she was a cracker. Probably married with kids by now – lucky bloke! He hoped that one day he'd meet a woman just like her, for she really was something special.

THE PERFECT MATCH

Helen closed the front door. There – husband gone to work and the children off to school for the day; what a relief. Oh dear, now she felt guilty for even feeling like that. But no matter how organised she tried to be, early mornings were always hectic. How on earth did mums with half a dozen children manage?

She went into the kitchen and switched on the jug. A coffee in the beautiful peace and quiet and then I'll get the washing on; but for now…

Helen sat and sipped her coffee. Three active children and a husband who never lent a hand sometimes got her down. But look on the bright side, she told herself. All of us have good health and the children are happy – well most of the time. The family enjoyed living in West Auckland's Green Bay, and the schools there were great. Still, she was glad of the part-time waitressing job she had three evenings a week; it gave her a break from the house and the money was needed. Always earmarked before she got it.

Smoocher rubbed himself around her legs as if to say 'I'm here, I care'. Helen bent down and hoisted up the oversized, gingernut-coloured cat for a cuddle.

There was a bone of contention with her husband Clive and the children at the moment. The children all wanted a dog and he sided with them. Helen thought that the cat, the finches, the guinea pigs and goldfish, were more than enough pets. Especially as she had to nag the

19

children to clean out said cages and fish bowl, and she was the one who always fed the cat.

Having finished her coffee, Helen put the purring cat down and got started on the household chores. Washing first, then beds and vacuuming, before she walked to the shops for a few food items.

Helen glanced out the window and soaked up the glorious sight of the furry buds of magnolias showing a peek of purple, and beneath them, a scattering of swelling daffodil heads confirmed that spring was on the way. Her spirits lifted.

The day sped by. The washing dried and she'd done the ironing, as well as sorting out the hot water cupboard. Always extras to do. She had the dinner pre-prepared before the children arrived home and there would be a batch of hot cheese scones ready for their snack. They always came home hungry!

The door slammed as the two youngest children walked in.

"How many times have I asked you not to slam doors?" Helen asked, and then to make up for growling the moment they walked in, ruffled their hair asking, "And how was school today?"

Jemma and Paula both talked at once – which was the norm for them. "Hold on, hold on, one at a time please," Helen said.

The girls were very close in age so shared the same class, as their teacher Miss Jenson took both year six and seven pupils. The big news today was a forthcoming school trip to a camp in the Waitakere Ranges.

"We can go, can't we Mum?" they chorused excitedly.

"Sounds good, but that will depend on the cost I suppose. We'll have to wait for more details from school and your father and I will need to discuss this. Now, go and wash your hands and then you can have some scones and milk."

Alex arrived home from College and with a shouted "Hi Mum," went through to his room to dump the heavily-laden backpack. Coming into the kitchen he gave his mum a quick hug before saying, "Cheese scones, beauty. I'm starving."

Looking at Jemma and Paula he asked, "How are you two goons?" Goons being his latest teasing name for his sisters. The tone for the rest of the afternoon was set.

It seemed no time at all before Helen heard the sound of a car and the children's yell. "Dad's home, Mum."

Helen looked at the kitchen clock as her husband Clive walked in. It was after six and he knocked off at four-thirty. She didn't have to ask where he'd been that extra hour; she could smell the beer.

"What's for dinner? I could eat a horse," he asked.

"I have work tonight," Helen told him. "So it's a casserole; vegies and all together. I'll be off soon, so you can dish up, and the kids will help. If it's quiet in the restaurant I could be home by nine, if not, it's anyone's guess."

She gave Clive a peck on the cheek and went to say goodbye to the children.

It was nearly eleven o'clock when Helen finally arrived home. Clive was sound asleep and didn't even sense her getting into bed. It seemed as if she'd only just fallen asleep when the alarm rang – six am. Another day beckoned. At least I don't have to work tonight, she thought. Clive and I should have time to talk about the school trip. She smiled as she recalled the $20.00 she'd earned in tips last night.

Clive left for work, and over breakfast Alex looked across the table at Helen and told her they were getting a dog. His sisters grinned smugly and nodded their heads.

"I beg your pardon," Helen said. "Did I hear right? Did you say we were getting a dog; and since when?"

"Since last night Mum," Alex answered. "There's this guy at Dad's work who's got a dog and needs to find a home for it. It's a cross between a Corgi and a Labrador. A real neat dog dad said, great with kids too."

"Hold it right there Alex," Helen said. "Your father hasn't discussed this with me yet, and anyway, I have already said no dog. We have enough animals as it is. Just forget it."

Helen saw the look pass between Alex and his sisters as he shrugged. "Think it's too late Mum. I reckon Dad's already made up his mind."

That morning after the children had left for school, Helen rang her friend and neighbour Pat. They arranged a morning coffee at Pat's place. Over coffee Helen unburdened her concerns. Pat always saw both sides of the story. But even she was shocked at the possibility of Clive making a decision to get a dog without even discussing it with his wife. Still, Helen felt better having told Pat. Just sharing this with her had helped.

The day dragged by. Helen only hoped the children had misunderstood their father.

The children arrived home from school, one by one. Each looked at her warily, keeping out of her way with the comment that there was heaps of homework to do today.

Helen sat in the lounge, thumbing through, but not really absorbing, the latest NZ Women's Weekly. Her mind was elsewhere.

The honk from a car caught her by surprise. She looked up to see Clive getting out of the station wagon and going to the back of the vehicle. Helen took a deep breath. Clive was pulling on a leash and coaxing a golden coloured dog to jump down.

Helen put hands to her face. Oh no! The kids were right. He had brought a dog home.

Then the girls burst out from their bedroom, closely followed by Alex. With cries of 'He's got him' and 'Oh, he's beautiful', they all rushed out to their father.

Helen knew there was nothing more to be said at this time. She just went to the kitchen and got on with cooking dinner. Whatever she said, she knew that to the children she was a spoilsport. Best to talk to Clive after the children were in bed.

Clive had already decided that until he got the dog a kennel, Butch, as the dog was named, would sleep in Alex's room. Apparently Alex was rapt with this.

Helen tried to stay calm as she pointed out to Clive the unfair way he had gone about getting the dog. Plus, there was the cost of a kennel. Was the dog registered? Had he been fixed? 'I'm not sure, I think so,' were the careless answers.

"Why did the guy at work not keep the dog?" Helen asked.

"They have a new baby and a toddler – the dog was just too much for his wife to handle. But don't worry

Helen, he'll be great with older kids, just you wait and see."

Wait and see Helen did.

Within a couple of weeks the novelty of having a dog began to wear off. For the children, walking the dog lost its attraction. Apparently Butch pulled on the lead and, tried to chase cats. He growled and snarled at other dogs, on leads or in their own properties. Alex was furious when he found half of a school assignment chewed into a soggy mess on his bedroom floor. The girls were missing items of clothing, some of which was found outside after days of rain, half-hidden in bushes or dug in a hole and roughly covered with mud.

Helen took over exercising Butch on her walks to the shops but he almost pulled her arms out of their sockets, he was so strong.

A kennel became urgent. The novelty of a snoring and as Alex soon found out – even worse – a farting dog as a sleeping companion, soon faded. Having heard of the dog's farting, the girls said a definite NO to having him in their room.

One lovely clear day Helen hung out the washing, thinking with the breeze and sun it would be dry in no time. A couple of hours later she looked out of the kitchen window to see the rotary clothesline going around and around like a spinning top. What the…!

She shot out onto the back deck. There was Butch, one of the big white sheets clamped in his jaws, running in circles, the unpegged end of the sheet dragging in the now muddy ground.

Helen ran down and walloped the dog's head and still he wouldn't let go. She went and turned on the hose and let him have it. That did the trick.

With a yelp he let go the washing, but then raced straight for the back door, Helen in hot pursuit. She only had to follow the muddy paw prints to find Butch, panting away and dripping water onto the middle of Alex's bed.

She dragged him by his collar and locked him in the garage. Let him stay there until his 'Master' came home. Helen sat at the table and thinking of the mess to clean up and the cost of new sheets, burst into tears.

It was another evening of recriminations. Clive said it was all Helen's fault. She should have checked that Butch was indoors before hanging out the washing. After all, he was still only a youngster, hadn't calmed down yet, give him time. Helen fumed.

A few days later Helen took out some schnitzel from the freezer and left it on the bench to thaw. She put a net cover over it in case of flies and went to get some ironing done. Finally with it all done and put away, she came back to the lounge to see Butch lying in the sun that streamed through the window. Helen thought, look at that, maybe he's settling down at last. She went into the kitchen to prepare the schnitzel and stopped. The plate on the bench was empty, the net cover knocked over and the floor smeared with blood. Not one piece of meat remained.

This time Helen didn't cry. She simply rang Clive at work, told him his dog had eaten their dinner and that on his way home he would have to pick up fish and chips. She then promptly hung up.

A week followed of watching the dog's every move. Clive still hadn't bought a kennel, had not even put up a running lead as suggested by Helen. So far, so good until...

Helen was in the dining room doing a repair job on a pair of Alex's school shorts. She had last seen Butch in the kitchen, asleep on the cool lino floor. Suddenly a flash of bright clothing went past the window. Helen stood to see the neighbour's daughter Ashley, racing after Butch, shouting as she ran. Butch had a very large piece of blood-dripping red meat in his jaws.

It took Helen and Ashley ages to corner the dog and prise the chunk of corned silverside from its mouth. They both agreed the meat was unusable.

Again Butch was locked in the garage where he howled and howled. Helen of course promised the neighbour she would replace the stolen meat. Maybe I didn't latch the back door properly, she wondered. In a way then, it's partly my fault.

Another night of accusations. Helen was told she had never wanted the dog – the dog sensed this and only did things for attention – what? But this time the children were quiet. They no longer stuck up for Butch. They just looked sad, remaining silent.

There were a few quiet days and then the weekend arrived and everything turned to custard.

Clive was tinkering with the car. Checking oil etc. and wondering if he could do an oil-change himself, when all hell broke loose. Butch had been in the garage with him. They lived on a fairly busy road so when a horn sounded Clive took little notice. Neither did Helen who was in the kitchen baking.

Then came a loud thumping on the front door. Helen, floury hands and all, went to see who it was. She was quite frightened by the red-faced irate man who shook his fists and shouted at her.

"Your bloody dog. I could've been killed. Ran right out in front of me he did. If I hadn't hit the kerb and straightened up, I would have gone right through your fence and into your house".

By this time Clive had arrived from the garage demanding to know what all the noise was about. The man continued to rave on.

"There were kids walking on the footpath too. Imagine, I could have killed them and all because of your bloody stupid dog. Know it was yours. Saw him shoot around the back. Here, I'll show you."

They all trooped to the back garden and sure enough there was Butch, tongue lolling and side heaving as if he had just run a marathon.

Helen didn't say a word. Just turned and went inside and left Clive to deal with the upset man. She was glad it was a Saturday. At least the children were out at their sports and didn't have to see or hear this.

Eventually Clive came inside. He and Helen talked quietly.

"Yes it has been a mistake," Clive admitted. "The man was right. The dog is a menace."

"Something has to be done," Helen said. "But you're the one who got the dog, so it has to be your decision. What do you think we should do?"

"Let me think about this overnight. I know he has to go. I'll sort something out, I promise. And Helen, I am so very, very sorry. I've been a darned fool."

They both had tears in their eyes as they looked down at the golden dog who looked up at them so trustingly.

"Not a word to the children till I've decided the best way to handle this, okay Helen?"

The next day a decision was made. A new home would be found for Butch. But done properly. Clive would put an advertisement in the NZ Herald for next Friday and Saturday's edition. As a result there were several phone calls from people enquiring about the dog who needed a home.

One in particular seemed the most suitable. It was from a Bob Walton, a recently retired school teacher who lived in the small but quaint town of Waihi. This town was well-known for having a goldmine still in operation. Bob was a widower and he'd been thinking of getting a dog for a while. A keen walker, he said he would enjoy the company of a dog and he had a fully fenced property, so the dog would have plenty of room to run around and be quite safe.

Helen and Clive liked the sound of him and made arrangements to take Butch down to meet him. A bit of a drive from Auckland, but that was okay. They wondered how the children would react to the news. Rather surprisingly they all thought it a good idea – as long as Butch was happy.

They had an uneventful run through to Waihi. Nearing the town they drove through the Karangahake Gorge. Quite an experience with a narrow road that twisted and turned. The children loved the spectacular sights of water foaming over enormous boulders in the gouged-out river, set off by towering granite cliffs, but

Helen was thankful to leave the darkness of the gorge and get back out into the sunlight.

Nearing the town, Clive pulled in. An avenue of stately palms led to the town centre. He checked his map. "Yep, I know just where to go now. About three more roads along, on the right. Then Bob Walton's street should be second on the left. He said it was an old house painted white, with a picket fence and a big red number 14 on the letterbox. Said we couldn't miss it."

A few minutes later they arrived. "Old house alright." commented Helen. "It's gorgeous. I bet it's one of the original miner's cottages." The children piled out and Alex went to get Butch, being careful to first clip on his lead.

"I'll just go and let the chap know we're here. Won't be a minute," Clive told them.

Even before he got to the gate, a man was approaching from the side of the house. They all watched as the two men shook hands.

"Come on you lot. Come and meet Mr. Walton," Clive called.

But first things first. The man stooped down to make a great fuss of Butch who had promptly sat when he was told, looking positively angelic. Mr. Walton – Bob to everyone he said, welcomed them into his home.

It was more than an hour before the family left Bob's house. They looked back at him standing at the gate with his new companion by his side. The two girls were a bit weepy, but soon got over it at the thought of lunch somewhere in the town. Alex was excited about viewing the open cast Martha mine that Bob Walton had told them about.

Alex, showing a wisdom beyond his age, summed up Butch and his new home nicely. "Back there is a happy dog and a happy man, the perfect match if you ask me."

A couple of weeks later Helen collected the mail from their letterbox. As she wandered back to the house she turned a letter over to check the sender. Well I'll be, she thought. Bob Walton. Showing great strength of will, she didn't open it, just left it on the mantelpiece. For when the family was there, to read together.

After Clive got home from work they sat at the table and Helen read out the letter.

Dear Clive, Helen and the children,

I just wanted to write and thank you properly for entrusting me with your dog. You inferred he could be a bit of a rascal. Well if he is, I have seen no sign of this. Within a few days he settled in to a routine which matches my own. He does not bark unless someone comes to the door and I am happy with that. He is like my shadow accompanying me wherever I go. I feed him in the kitchen, and he even stops eating his food to follow me if I leave the room. Of an evening he curls up on the old settee next to me, and appears to enjoy television. When I work in the vegetable garden he lies in the shade of the oak tree always with one eye on me. I move – he moves. I have found he enjoys the beach and is a strong swimmer. We have already had some splendid walks and have many more planned.

I could not ask for a more devoted companion. Just one thing. I do hope you don't mind. I have given him a new name. Butch sounded too rough for such a well-behaved dog, so I have called him Major.

He does seem to be happy with that and immediately comes when called. Acceptance of the name I think.

Thank you again, from both myself and Major.

Regards,

Bob Walton.

MEANT TO BE

After four years working at Giles Engineering, a fourth salary increase and another generous bonus gave Emma a strong feeling of independence. She had deferred going to Uni as she was strongly averse to taking on a student loan. Her folks had offered to pay her fees, but owing money in any way at all, was not for Emma. She would rather go to Uni when she could afford to do so, even if that meant waiting a few years.

The men at work couldn't quite make her out. In appearance Emma was a real cracker. A Rachel Hunter type they reckoned, being tall and having a curvy body that the plainest of clothes couldn't hide. No blonde hair though. Emma's hair was long and straight, with the sheen of rich dark grapes. She was friendly with her warm smile, but made it clear she was not for touching – or chatting up. Somehow a cool look from those deep blue eyes was enough, and the guys soon learnt to keep their distance.

It was just before her twenty-second birthday that Emma began to have thoughts of moving out from home. Not because she wasn't happy there; her folks were super considerate and never kept tabs on her, and her two brothers weren't too bad. It was just …

The need to spread her wings and fly, to prove to herself she could live independently. A new challenge in the new millennium.

Her parents, Beth and Ron, were very busy people, both in demanding jobs. A lot of their home time was spent ferrying Emma's younger brothers to sports interests. To help out, Emma took over many of the household chores, including much of the cooking. In return for her help, and as money was not an issue for Beth and Ron, she didn't pay board.

A love of figures was what had got Emma the job at Giles. She had taken on the role of accounts manager with amazing confidence for one so young, even putting in place changes which worked to the advantage of the business; much to the pleasure of the firm's accountant. Hence the top salary and bonuses. She had her Dad's shrewd way with money and loved to see her bank balance steadily increase. Her only major spending was in buying her wee car. Even that had been a bargain, bought from a friend heading to Oz to live.

Sometimes, on a Friday after work, Emma met her old college friend Lyn for a drink at the corner bar in Grey Lynn. They liked the good vibes of the place, the soft music and in summer, the beer garden where they would sit under the big shade sails. The majority of men who went there were well dressed. No scruffs or rowdies to be seen, or heard – nice.

After leaving College Lyn had gone straight into a hairdressing apprenticeship, and every time they met Emma noted she sported a new hair colour or style. Lyn was as vibrant as her appearance with a bubbly outgoing nature; the perfect foil for Emma's rather quiet ways. Today, streaks of a plummy colour ran through Lyn's blonde hair and a rebellious ruby nose-stud glittered in the sun.

As they entered the bar Emma spotted the 'man with the reddish beard' as she had come to think of him. She'd seen him a few times and he stood out, not just because of his strikingly masculine appearance, but because he dressed more casually and always drank alone. On this particular evening he gave the girls a slight smile and nodded pleasantly.

As they took their drinks out to the beer garden Lyn asked. "Do you know that guy with the beard Em? He seemed to be looking at you."

"Only from seeing him here, and I think he was nodding to both of us, not just me."

That evening Emma talked to Lyn about her thoughts of leaving home. Lyn didn't seem at all surprised asking, "Where would you go, what sort of a place would you look for? Flat sharing, an apartment or what?" She looked quizzically at Emma.

"I don't really know till I look I suppose. Cost will decide that, but my dream would be to have a wee house of my own. You know I'm pretty careful with money. Well I think I might have enough for a deposit on a basic house and if I'm going to become a home owner it had better be now. Prices have started going up and I reckon now is the time to buy. I think flatting is just money down the drain and I don't know how I would get on sharing with strangers. I'd love to have a dog too, and as the last accounts manager had one sitting in her office, I guess I could take it to work with me. I'd have to check of course," she mused. "I don't care if a property needs work, I'd love a do-up, and I'm pretty good with a paint brush. Remember how I tarted up my room? Did the papering and all, nothing to it." Emma grinned at Lyn. "Well, what do you think."?

"It seems to me that your mind is already made up. Main thing I see is cost. You've got me wishing I hadn't always spent so much on clothes and my neat car. I'll be paying that off for another year, damn it! Comes of being a hairdresser I guess, looks are just so important. Anyway Em, have you talked to your folks about this yet?"

"No, I haven't." Emma frowned. "I've been worried sick about how they will take my moving out. You know Mum relies on me a lot and I don't want to hurt her, or Dad's, feelings. I'm not looking forward to telling them. I thought of taking them out for dinner and talking to them then. I feel shitty about the whole thing and just hope they'll understand."

"Of course they'll understand," Lyn reassured her. "Taking them out for a meal is a great idea. What about that new Asian restaurant in Kingsland? The girls at work have all been and say it's great. The food and, prices too Miss Stingy," and she laughed at Emma screwing up her face.

"Talking of wasting money, it's time we headed for home; come on Lyn." And saying thanks to the pleasant young barman they left the bar.

When Emma's parents heard she was taking them out to dinner they were delighted and looked forward to a night of, as her Mum put it, 'No cooking or cleaning up to do for either of us.'

The meal was as good as they had hoped and once desserts were served along with lovely coffees and liqueurs, Emma broached the subject of her possible move.

"There's something I want to talk to you about." She took a deep breath. "I have been thinking about this for a while. I do hope you won't be upset, but I really would like to find a place of my own. Maybe a flat or a small apartment. I don't really know what, until I've had a look. You know I've been saving ever since I started work, and never touched my bonuses. Well, I hope I may even have enough for a deposit on a house. Providing it's in my price range that is. What do you think – Mum, Dad?"

Emma watched her parents look first at each other, and then back at her. Relief flooded through her as they both smiled. At a tacit nod of agreement from her mum, her dad was the first to speak.

"Emma sweetheart, Mum and I are very proud that you've worked so hard and done so well. We knew this day would come so it's really no surprise. Of course we would miss you terribly. But we'll help you in any way we can, won't we Beth? Perhaps a little help with the deposit if there's a bit of a shortfall?"

"Of course Ron," her mother added. "We'll always be there to help. Oh dear! Why am I weepy? Silly me. Only one thing, Emma love. Please don't go too far away from us."

Emma reached across the table and held her mother's hand. "That's an easy promise to make Mum, and thanks Dad for the offer, I'll certainly need your advice and Mum's help. Just think – it will be great fun looking at properties, who knows what we'll find."

"Let's drink to that," said her dad.

Emma sat back, relaxed at last, and lifted her glass. "Here's to house-hunting. Cheers Dad, cheers Mum, and thanks for understanding."

Over the next few months Emma looked at many properties. The house market in Auckland was a real eye-opener. She kept in mind that this would be just a foot in the door. She was not afraid of hard work, so long as the place was sound. So far however there was nothing within her price range.

Emma had often heard her mum say 'It's not what you know, but who you know.' She found this to be right, when one Saturday morning Lyn phoned. She told Emma that since her grandma had passed away about a year ago, her parents had been renting out the old family home. With all the legal work finalised they were going to put the house on the market. Gran had done very little to the old house in recent years, always saying it was fine the way it was. In reality there was some roofing and weatherboards to replace, window sashes that needed fixing and the kitchen and bathroom sure needed updating. Lyn remembered wobbly steps too. The good news was that it wasn't far from where Emma's folks lived.

"I mentioned to Mum and Dad that you're looking for a place. Would you like to talk to them and have a look at the house? What do you reckon?" she asked Emma. "And being close to Grey Lynn Park," she added, "it's handy for walking a dog!"

Emma could tell Lyn was grinning. Her stomach did an excited flip. "Would I what? Oh Lyn, yes please. I'll ring them straight away."

Emma's parents went with her to view the house, her mum with notebook at the ready.

They met Lyn's father, Dan, at the property. The house was a square-fronted villa with a veranda and a central front door. It certainly did have a neglected appearance. The picket fence was wobbly and as they walked around to the back door Emma saw the pathway needed replacing. Lyn had been right about the steps too and Emma dodged what she thought was a rotting board. Layers of paint peeled from around the windows and even Emma's untrained eye spotted some rotting weatherboards. But not in the least daunted, she followed Dan into the house.

A list was made of obvious repairs and Dan was happy for Emma's dad to organise a builder, plumber etc. to check it all out. A LIM report would be needed too. Emma found she had a lot to learn. Then came the discussion on price. Allowances would be made for work needed, and the money saved by both parties in not having to pay Real Estate agents' fees.

Emma felt an instant affinity for the old place. Saw it as it could be, not as it was now. The back garden could be easily fenced off for a dog! And there was a lemon tree and a couple of other fruit trees too. Super shady spots for summer. Yes, the house sure did need work, but she had all the time in the world. She began to get really excited but knowing she shouldn't appear too keen, wisely kept quiet and let her dad do the talking.

Later in the day Lyn called in to ask Emma, "What did you think of Gran's place? A bit of work needed eh? Anyway that's not the only thing I wanted to ask you. All your plans got me thinking. It really is time I left the nest too. I wonder if you would consider me as a house-mate. Before you say anything Em, I'd expect to pay my fair share and we do get on well; so would you think about it? That is, if you do end up buying the house. Hey, I just thought, that would be a good point when going for a mortgage too wouldn't it? The extra money coming in, I mean."

Emma gave Lyn a hug. "That's something I never expected. But let's wait and see what happens. It may be that I would have a job getting a loan on the house. As Dad would say, don't count your chickens before they're hatched."

Emma was to learn that when it comes to buying a property, things take time. But within a month everything began to fall into place. The old house proved to have good solid bones, the LIM report was okay, and after checking Emma's banking record and her income, the BNZ were happy to provide a home loan. Negotiations with Lyn's dad had been settled to both parties' satisfaction. Knowing Lyn wanted to share with Emma had really swung the deal.

The two young women stood in the middle of the lounge and looked about them. "It's mine," Emma shouted, flinging her arms out wide in a most un-Emma-like way. Happy laughter echoed in the bare room. "Let's figure out what furniture we need." And the planning began.

Three months later the girls were well and truly settled in. They both brought some furniture from home and then trawled second-hand outlets looking for bargains.

Emma delighted in this, knocking prices down to the lowest amount possible. A big old oak dresser, a comfy settee, and oak coffee table plus a well-worn dining table with four chairs were their major purchases. Lyn provided a couple of bean chairs and the music, with her CD set-up in the lounge, and in one corner, they hung Emma's TV given to her by her parents. Lyn's folk contributed a couple of big floor rugs, one for her bedroom and one which made the lounge cosy. Both mums had cleaned out their kitchen cupboards and given the girls unwanted crockery, cutlery and pots. Gran's old washing machine and fridge/freezer had been left as part of the chattels. They would do for now. And between them the girls' dads organised to mow the lawns – all sorted.

Emma and Lyn got back into a routine of work and weekends. Lyn often had a date on a Saturday night – sometimes the date rolling into Sunday. Fine as far as Emma was concerned, and she quite enjoyed having the house to herself occasionally. She had dated a few times, but really wasn't interested in all that palaver. Perhaps having brothers had put her off! Anyway she was only young. Maybe later, who knew?

Emma got back into jogging. Throughout her school years she had enjoyed running, especially cross-country. She had been a bit lax of late, but now, after work, she would take off for a good half-hour run. At weekends, being an early riser she tended to go in the mornings.

As she ran along the neighbourhood streets, Emma thought again how good it would be to have a dog with her. She decided the first step was to ask if she could take a dog to work. If the answer was yes, the second step would be to get a fence built across the back of the house. She was sure that both Dan and her dad, being handy with a hammer, could be relied on to tackle that.

The answer at work was, 'Okay as long as it is well behaved.'

Emma and Lyn asked their dads for help. They got stuck in and in no time the fence was up, complete with a lockable side gate. Emma thought it added to the house rather nicely, the menfolk having built a picket style fence to match up with the front. And they repaired the wobbly front fence at the same time. Wonderful to have dads!

Now that the property was 'dog proof' Emma went to the local RSPCA seeking an unwanted, but she hoped loveable, dog. She walked along the kennel runs to a chorus of gruff barks and high-pitched yaps. Some dogs lunged at the fences, some scratched at the wire for attention, and it was all very confusing.

"Do you have any particular sort of dog in mind?" the attendant asked her.

"No, though I think I'll know when I see it – or hear it."

She was wrong with the last comment. They walked past several runs and Emma felt a bit guilty but none of the dogs appealed. Then a bit further along there was this dog. All alone, it sat on its haunches quietly, just looking towards her. Emma saw big, sad, brown eyes, one circled by a large cream loop of fur, and unmatched dark brown ears, one floppier than the other. The dog stood and Emma watched as it walked towards her. It stopped at the fence and, head to one side, raised a paw. For Emma it was an epiphany of instant love. The dog had made the decision.

Loopy, Emma called her. It suited the odd-coloured patch of hair and seemed to match her nature. Loopy was a mix of Labrador and something unknown, an average sized gentle bitch who would prove to be Emma's best friend. Best of all, Loopy loved to run.

The morning was clear, crisp and cold, with a heavy dew. The skies fingered with white streaks among the watery blue. One of those few precious days when sun shone intermittently, and you longed for summer.

Emma dressed in a tracksuit and finished tying her sneakers. Quietly she let herself and Loopy out of the house and through the gates. After a late night Lyn was still sleeping soundly. Emma attached Loopy's lead to her collar. Tail wagging excitedly, and paws bouncing up and down on the path, the dog was eager to go. Emma ran slowly at first, loosening up tight limbs. Her long hair was pulled up into a ponytail and without a scrap of makeup she had the fresh sparkling appearance of natural beauty.

Loopy was getting to know the usual route and seemed confused when Emma said, "Come on girl, let's go this way for a change," turning in to a tree-lined avenue. The peace of early morning never ceased to soothe Emma. For a while she felt as if she had the world to herself until a small yappy dog broke the silence as it raced to the gate, telling Loopy to go away.

The road began to slope upwards and Emma slowed down. They topped the rise and here the road levelled out. The houses were similar to hers, mostly villas, though much grander. Wide verandas and brightly coloured glass fronted doors shone in welcome.

Further ahead Emma saw a tall man washing a car, the sun showing up the red of his hair. As Emma drew closer a feisty black cat leapt out from a driveway to spit at Loopy. Loopy reacted by swinging towards the cat and the leash tangled around Emma's legs. Down she went, sprawling hard onto the footpath.

"Shit!" Feeling a fool she looked to see if anyone had seen, or heard her. Loopy wasn't helping by licking her face, and as Emma tried to unwind herself from the leash she heard a man's voice.

Emma looked up to see the man with the reddish beard! Jeez, did she feel an idiot. He reached down to help her up.

"Are you all right? That was an awful tumble you took." He gazed at Emma with a look of concern and took Loopy's leash from her. As Emma stood up, it was obvious she would not be running home. Her knees were bleeding and she felt unsteady. Another look from those sea green eyes had her most confused. Her heart raced. Must be the fall, she thought, and took the hand he offered.

"Thank you, I feel so stupid. It was the cat you see."

"I've seen you at the corner bar haven't I?" he asked. "Sorry, I'm Pete Wintle. Can I help you along to my place and we'll get those knees of yours cleaned up. Then maybe a cuppa to settle you down. You've had a nasty shock. If you like, I'll drive you home later. There's plenty of room in the old station wagon for your dog." And without waiting for an answer, Pete led her towards his house.

Emma sat in the kitchen trying not to be a sook as he gently sponged her knees. Loopy sat comfortingly next to her, seeming quite at home. In a very short time Emma found out Pete liked dogs, he had a small workshop where he ran a furniture restoring business, and he had bought his house a few years ago. Like Emma, he was unattached.

Pete was most impressed at Emma having bought her own home, and very keen to have a look at the pieces of old furniture she had chosen. He laughed when Emma explained how Loopy had chosen her, but understood. When Pete found out where Emma worked, it turned out that one of the guys at Giles was an old friend of his, from working out at the gym. Small world, they agreed.

With her knees cleaned up and a coffee to sip, Emma felt much better. She sat back and caressed Loopy's ears. Amazing, she mused. Pete likes old houses, and old furniture–of course. And dogs!

As she gazed at Pete and he smiled at her, Emma's heart sped up a notch. A feeling of warmth flooded through her body. She wanted to reach out, to touch. She shook her head to stop these runaway thoughts, then realised she was happy with how she felt. This time her racing heart had nothing whatsoever to do with the fall.

Loopy padded over to Pete and leaned her head against him. She liked him too. That settled it for Emma. She smiled back at Pete as her last barrier came crashing down. This felt so right, Emma knew. This was meant to be.

OUT OF THE STORM

The wintry storm was reaching a crescendo when the door to the inn opened with a bang. The two men sitting at the bar and the woman serving them stared at the young women that staggered in.

They stood shivering; water dripping from saturated jackets, long hair plastered into submission. Both carried overstuffed zip-bags and dropped these on the floor with a thud. Apart from one girl being taller they could have been twins. Their wide eyes, the colour of sea-green rock pools, darted warily around the room.

"Bloody hell," one of the men muttered.

"That's not a very nice greeting Jack," the woman scolded. "Go on over to the fire, girls, and get those sodden jackets and boots off. I'll get you some towels." She hurried away. Within minutes she was back. "There, you dry yourselves and I'll get you a drink. What'll it be? Top shelf I expect to warm you up?"

The girls looked at each other. "Yeah, don't mind if we do, eh Holly," the tallest one said. "Rum and Coke and make it doubles, thanks."

"You girls picked the right place to stop. Mavis is like a mother hen, she'll look after you," the other man told them. He chuckled. "By the way, I'm Alf."

Years later Jack and Alf would re-tell the tale of the last of the winter storms in 2005 that brought Holly and Tammy to the Welcome Rest Inn at Partou Bay. "You

45

could tell they were good lookers, even drenched to the skin like they were." And they'd both nod in agreement.

The Welcome Rest Inn was unique; at least the small local population thought so. It had been a run-down seaside pub before Mavis and her husband Bob bought it, but they'd seen the potential. The last publican had been, like some others before him, too fond of a drop of the good stuff himself. Drank the profits, more's the shame.

To look at, Mavis and Bob were different as chalk and cheese. Because she was short and a little on the chubby side, Mavis had always looked older than she was. These days, the salt and pepper hair, along with a few more lines, confirmed her age. Still, when she smiled with those sparkling blue eyes people took an instant liking to her. Bob was of average height, all muscle and not a scrap of fat. There was Croatian in his family history and it showed. In summer his light brown skin tanned to a rich dark brown. His parents had told him he had his grandfather's eyes – bronzy-gold, the colour of streaked kauri gum.

They'd retired early after Bob sold out his partnership in the building trade. Not having had children they were free to suit themselves as to when, and what, they did. One weekend Bob had hitched the boat onto the SUV, and they'd left for a few days' fishing in the Bay of Islands. On their way up north they had taken a different route for a change, and stopped at the Welcome Rest Inn. Before they left, the 'For Sale' sign by the door got them thinking.

On their way home they stopped off again for another look. Eventually, after a lot of talking, they decided to put in a 'silly' offer for the Inn. For the last ten years Mavis had worked as a barmaid at their local RSA. She had a great head for figures too. Bob could see where improvements could be made in the building. And although he didn't say so to Mavis, he looked forward to having his own boat ramp, fishing whenever he wanted. The Inn was a challenge for them both. They only enjoyed the occasional drink so there'd be no chance of them drinking the profits!

Over the next couple of years, Bob's building improvements and Mavis's flair for furnishings changed the Inn into a popular drinking spot and place to stay. The upstairs accommodation was improved with the addition of another guest bathroom. Bob also built coffee and tea making areas in each of the four double rooms. Mavis was sensible enough to offer a cooked breakfast only. According to liquor laws there had to be food available when selling alcohol, so there were always hot pies available from the warmer as well as the usual crisps and nuts. In the village, the local fish-shop and two cafés already provided meals and that worked well.

The girls' arrival changed a lot of things. They never said where they were from, just the 'big smoke'. So, Auckland probably. But that was their business. They'd been hitchhiking their way around the north apparently, getting work wherever they could. Capable of turning their hands to most things, including pulling a pint, they'd told Mavis and Bob. With the busiest time of the year fast approaching, the timing of their arrival was perfect. Being right by the beach with safe swimming and great fishing to be had, the inn was getting very popular.

Within a few days of their arrival, Mavis gave Holly a job as barmaid and employed Tammy as assistant housekeeper. Only a few hours a day for both of them, but with free board they were happy with that. Best of all, they could sunbathe and swim every day the sun shone – spot on! They settled in and it seemed like the girls might be staying for a while.

One day Mavis and Bob stood on the lawn that led from the inn, down to the beach. "Like flipping porpoises aren't they Bob?" Mavis commented. "Like they were born in the sea."

"Must have grown up somewhere by the beach to swim like that," Bob agreed. "Odd the way they never talk about their past lives, but they're good workers, and honest. As far as I'm concerned that's all that matters."

"Have you noticed young Aaron Spedding is coming in more often of late?" Mavis asked. "I reckon he's getting keen on Holly."

"Well, Holly is a rather stunning looking girl."

"Noticed, have you?" and Mavis gave Bob a teasing nudge.

"Get off the grass girl, you know she's young enough to be my daughter." Bob looked away as if embarrassed.

He is funny at times, Mavis thought.

Christmas was looming and every room in the inn was booked. "A bit like that first Christmas." Mavis was heard to quip. "No room at the inn!"

One morning Mavis said she needed to go into Kerikeri to buy some new bed linen, towels and table settings. She'd look at replacing some of the dining room cutlery also. She thought of staying a night or two with her friend Julie.

"Can you and the girls manage without me for a couple of nights?" She asked Bob. "I'd like to stay over with Julie. I haven't seen her for ages."

"Not a problem," Bob said. "After all, we managed with just the two of us before the girls arrived, didn't we? Anyway, the break will do you good."

So it was arranged, and a few days later Mavis left for Kerikeri.

She got home full of chatter about Julie and her family, and the couple of restaurant meals they'd enjoyed. And how the town had grown even more since her last trip there. She'd had a great time. Mavis found Bob a bit quiet, but then he never was a great talker. Not like she was.

Holly and Tammy were working full-time now, and Bob and Mavis were jolly glad to have them. Bob had built table and chair seating on the back lawn, where you could sit and look out to sea. Sun umbrellas were up and this new outdoors spot was well patronised. Tammy rushed in and out, taking and bringing orders from the bar. She and Holly were proving popular and did well with tips, especially as the drinks continued to flow.

Bob wisely offered a shuttle service, keeping an eye on the level of drinking, and checking the ages of the young ones from the motor camp at the other end of the bay.

Summer came with a vengeance, hitting the high twenties. According to news reports the hottest summer yet was expected.

One afternoon when Mavis walked into the kitchen, she was concerned to see Holly, head in hand, sitting at the table.

"What's wrong Holly?" she asked. "Are you alright, is the heat getting to you?" Going to the fridge Mavis poured her a tall glass of water. "There now, drink that and sit quietly for a while."

"Thanks, sorry to be a nuisance," Holly muttered. "I just came over all wobbly. I'll be all right in a minute. Bob will be waiting for me to take over the bar."

Later that day, as had become the norm, Aaron Spedding waited for Holly to knock off work, then off they went. You could hear his truck start up from inside the bar. "Wonder he gets away with that noisy bloody muffler," someone commented.

"They make them noisy on purpose these days," an old codger at the leaner said.

"Leave them be," another joined in. "You were young once – if you can remember that far back!"

Even the old codger laughed at that.

In bed one night Mavis looked up from her book and asked Bob, "Have you noticed Tammy seems very quiet these days? I wonder if she's got her nose out of joint now Holly's going steady with young Aaron." After a minute or so with no answer forthcoming, she asked again. "Well Bob, what do you think?"

"I think woman, that you should read your book and let me read mine in peace. You imagine things, that's all."

At last the summer rush eased off and life went back to an easier pace. Mavis insisted the girls take a bonus for all their hard work, saying that without them they couldn't have coped.

Bob had been touchy for some time, and now he was really edgy – short-tempered and seemingly reluctant to work in the bar. He pottered outside mostly, replacing the odd weatherboard, painting and gardening.

Mavis wondered if Bob had been overdoing it. She felt a bit that way herself lately. Maybe they should start planning a holiday; even a few days away would be nice. Go down to Auckland, take in a show and catch up with family and a few old friends. But when she suggested this to Bob he didn't seem interested. In fact he seemed really annoyed. Mavis thought, 'Shit. What else can I do?'

She was in the bar one morning doing a stock-take, when Holly arrived. As the girl lifted the hatch to come behind the bar, Mavis noticed her turn slightly sideways to walk through the narrow opening. She couldn't mistake the bump. Holly was very definitely pregnant!

Later on Mavis went looking for Bob. She found him outside, putting a new coat of Kwila stain on some of the wooden furniture.

"Bob, we need to talk," Mavis began.

"What's the problem now?" Bob asked, frowning.

"Well, the problem is really Holly's. I've only just noticed, but I'm sure the girl's pregnant."

Bob stopped working and glanced briefly at Mavis. Going on with his staining he said, "Well, these things do happen you know. She's not a kid and she's been going out with that Aaron chap for months now." He shrugged. "Anyway, what do you expect me to do about it?"

"Hang on Bob. I'm worried about the girl, and don't you feel some sort of responsibility for her welfare? I mean, those girls do live under our roof."

"That doesn't make me their keeper, and you need to remember, you're not their bloody mother either," Bob muttered. "Now let me get on with this job."

Mavis hated the waiting. When would Holly come and tell her and Bob about her situation? The atmosphere became very strained, until several days later, Tammy and Holly came in to the kitchen wanting a word with Mavis. Tammy was the one to break the silence.

"Holly's pregnant, Mavis. She's going to live with Aaron Spedding. She feels awful about letting you down though. Isn't that right Holly?"

Holly could hardly look Mavis in the eye. She simply said, "Yes, this isn't something I wanted, but Aaron will look after me."

Mavis exploded. "So he damn well should. I'm sorry Holly. Sorry you're in this mess, but it does happen, we all know that." She reached over to give Holly a cuddle and Holly, pushing her away, burst into tears and rushed from the room.

Holly left to live with Aaron. Mavis couldn't help but wonder what she saw in him. A wish-washy sort if you asked her, with absolutely no personality. Ginger hair and freckles, skinny and pale. Oh well, no accounting for taste and they do say love is blind. But she did feel sorry for the girl.

Tammy seemed at a loose end without her friend, but being kept busy with both her own and Holly's jobs helped. Bob's humour hadn't improved and Mavis was not happy. For some unknown reason the enjoyment she and Bob used to share in running the inn had gone.

It came as no surprise to Mavis when a couple of months later Bob told her he wanted the business sold. He'd had enough. What Mavis wanted didn't seem to count as far as Bob was concerned; it was time for them to retire.

Their regulars were most upset. Old Jack and Alf told them they'd turned the place around. It was a real pleasure to drink there now. They joked that it had taken them a long time to get used to them. Now they'd have to start training new owners all over again!

Not surprisingly, the business sold quickly and Mavis and Bob moved on to the Kaipara Harbour area where they were nearer to Auckland, though still close to the sea for Bob's fishing.

Holly walked into the inn with her new baby son in her arms. She had come to see Tammy and to show the baby off. The menfolk made polite noises, but after Holly left it was Jack and Alf who voiced their opinions.

"Where the heck does that boy get his looks from?" Jack said. "He's olive skinned and those eyes, an odd sort-of brown. Makes me think of a small piece of polished kauri gum I've got at home. Bonny little kid mind, not skinny like his father."

"He sure isn't like Holly either," Alf added. "Must be a throwback. Mind you, kids change as they grow up, and he might too."

Thank God that's over, Tammy thought. She took a deep breath. "Anyone for another drink?" The answering clamour of orders settled, the men went back to their preferred topics of rugby, racing and of course, fishing. Much more interesting to men than blooming babies!

Almost eight years later, a slimmer, dark-haired, and very smartly dressed Mavis got out of her car. She stood in the carpark looking up at the sign, 'Welcome Rest Inn'. Still the same. Walking around to the back of the building she sat on one of Bob's wooden benches and looked out to the far horizon. Stroking the table, she thought how sad it had been that Bob had died before they'd come back for a last look. Over the last years Bob had seemed to settle down. Even bought her a little car of her own and welcomed old friends to stay. We never got the old spark back though, Mavis pondered; but we were content enough.

She got up, wandered down to the beach, and sat on the sea-wall enjoying the beautiful breeze. There were a few family groups about, some at the water's edge or in the sea. A couple of young boys were fooling around with a soccer ball. Suddenly there was a shout of 'watch it' and before Mavis could move, the ball landed whack against her legs. One of the boys raced across and picked up the ball.

"Jeez, I'm sorry lady. Are you okay?"

Mavis looked at the boy, for a moment unable to answer. "Yes, I'm fine thank you." Her heart raced. There was no mistaking the child's looks. Not only his looks but the way he stood, with a wide legged stance and his head slightly tilted to one side. Mavis looked into his eyes and knew for sure. The answer to the question she'd harboured all those years and never dared to ask Bob.

Mavis watched him re-join his mate, and misty eyed, turned away from the beach back to her car. She continued on the journey to visit her old friend Julie. She would never come back here again. Bob's secret would remain safe for the sake of his beautiful son.

HELL FIRE & DAMNATION

As soon as the child woke she remembered it was the special day of the week – Sunday. She heard the sound of gentle breathing, and turned to look at the still form of her sister Maisie in the other narrow bed.

Their room was very small, the beds separated only by a low set of drawers. Thin curtains covered a single sash window, doing little to prevent the early morning light. When windy, the curtains blew in and out as air came in through sneaky gaps in the wooden window frame. These the girls stuffed with cardboard and when they moaned to their dad about it, he told them to 'toughen up' as a bit of fresh air was good for them.

Across one corner a curtain hung from a wooden rod, forming a makeshift wardrobe, and on the back of the door two hooks held their dressing gowns, one pink, one blue. Under each bed a battered old suitcase held their woollens, along with heaps of stinky mothballs. Lots of other things got stuffed under the beds and regularly forgotten about.

A central light hung from the high board and batten ceiling. When turned on, a raggedy old fringed shade cut even more light from the miserly forty-watt lightbulb. This didn't stop the girls from reading in bed though.

When it was blowing a gale you could see the wallpaper move in and out. When they'd first moved in to the old house, the walls were only horizontal boards. Over the boards, a thin covering called scrim was kept in place with strips of tape pinned in a criss-crossed fashion. Wilma had been really excited when Mum told her that Dad would soon paper the walls.

"Will it be pretty paper, Mum?" she'd asked.

"That will depend on the cost of the paper I expect," her mother had said. "I just hope your father lines the walls first, that would make the room so much warmer. But you know, we should be thankful we have a home and your dad. After all, it's only three years since the war finished and he came home; bless him. We can't expect too much."

The wallpaper went up, but over the old scrim and the paper looked wobbly, not nice, and being a plain cream, not even pretty. So very disappointing, but Wilma reminded herself of her mother's words.

Lifting her head from the pillow Wilma listened. Yes, the tell-tale creaks of floorboards would be Dad coming down the hall on his way to the bathroom. She lay waiting for his morning call. I know where Mum will be, Wilma thought, at morning communion. She says she enjoys that and the singing most of all.

Wilma sighed, wishing the day didn't include going to Sunday school, then Sundays would be perfect.

"Come along girls," called her father as he popped his head around the door. "Sunday school for you two, your mother should be home soon."

Maisie's head appeared from beneath the bedclothes. She moaned to Wilma. "Blooming Sundays, I'll be glad when I'm older and don't have to go to Sunday school anymore. I'm thirteen next month. I wonder if that's old enough to get confirmed, then I could go to church with Mum instead. I'd much rather that than daft old Sunday school." She pulled the bedclothes over her head to snuggle back down.

Wilma got up and put on her dressing gown and slippers. Then quick as a flash she reached down and ripped the bedclothes off Maisie.

"You little creep," Maisie yelled. "Wait till I get you." Too late, for Wilma had already fled.

In the kitchen Wilma poured a glass of milk into a pot and clicked on a gas burner. Hot Milo coming up, now for toast.

Her dad, also in dressing gown and warm slippers, joined her. "Is Maisie up yet?"

"I think she would be, Dad." Wilma smirked. "Can I get you a cup of tea?"

"That would be nice love, and while you're at it, cut me a couple of slices of bread too will you. Hey! Watch your toast girl, it's smoking."

Wilma opened the toaster doors and rescued her toast. "That's okay Dad, I like it well done."

Maisie wandered in rubbing her eyes. Glaring at her sister she said, "One of these days I'll get you Wilma Tremore, see if I don't. Maybe cold water over you early one morning? How would you like that?"

Their father admonished the girls. "I don't know what this is all about you two, and I don't want to know. Could we just have breakfast in peace, please!"

Bruce Tremore gazed fondly at his daughters. The two girls were very alike. Both had his colouring, with hair a soft sandy shade and fair skin. He was pleased they had beautiful golden brown eyes just like their mother. Better than his wish-washy pale blue eyes, he always thought.

Breakfast was soon over and the girls had just finished dressing when they heard their father saying, "Hello there Jeanie love, how was church? Feeling holier than thou now are we?"

Removing her gloves and hanging her hat on the hallstand, Jean shook her dark curls free and chastised him. "You watch yourself Bruce, just because you seldom go to church is no reason to be smart. As a matter of fact I did have a very enjoyable time. Met the new leader of the 'Boys' Life Brigade' too. He seems a really nice man."

As Bruce raised his eyebrows at her last comment Jean added, "And his wife Nancy was there too, so don't look silly." She laughed at him. "Now, are the girls ready to leave? I'll just go and get out of these good clothes and then get started on the Sunday roast."

The girls joined their mother in the bedroom.

"Mum," Maisie began. "Wilma and I have been talking. Do we really have to keep going to Sunday school? Neither of us likes it. I get bored stiff with Mrs. Bender's rambling on and it's even worse for Wilma. Old Mr. Henderson scares her witless with all his gory bible stories."

"Yes Mum," Wilma chimed in. "Mr. Henderson stands there and scowls down at us like he's really angry. He puts on funny spectacles and they slip down his big nose and his eyes burn right into me. He shouts when he reads as if we kids are deaf and shakes his fingers at us. I don't think he likes us at all and the stories he tells are awful. There's always someone dying or going to be killed. Even temples crashing down on people and brothers killing each other, and babies being killed by soldiers. Mr. Henderson shows us this big book with coloured pictures and some of them are horrible."

"Alright, that's enough girls," their mother said. "I'll discuss this with your father and we will all talk about it when you get home. Now, off you go, and behave yourselves." Giving the girls a quick kiss she ushered them out the door.

With the midday meal over and the girls having done the dishes, the family sat at the table to sort out Maisie's questions and discuss the problem of Wilma not wanting to go to Sunday school.

As a result, Maisie now knew that yes, she would be confirmed after her next birthday and then she could go to church with her mother, no more Sunday school. Maisie was all smiles.

As to Wilma's problems, this would need to be handled very carefully. No way could they risk offending Mr. Henderson, but both parents felt it wrong for children to be frightened when learning about Jesus. After all, this should be a time of joyful learning. A visit to Mr. Henderson would be arranged and the matter discussed. Wilma was to go with them of course.

A week later, a worried Wilma held her mother's hand tightly as they drew close to the Henderson's house. They walked through the iron gateway up the brick path to the front door. It was Mrs Henderson who made them welcome. She was the exact opposite of her husband, very short and comfortably rounded. She beamed at them as she led them into the parlour.

"My husband is in his study," she told them. "He works so hard for the good of the parish. I'll get him for you. Please, do have a seat."

After a few minutes Mr. Henderson entered the room. He was a tall, lean man with angular, rather severe features and piercing dark brown eyes. He greeted his visitors pleasantly enough then asked, "In what way can I be of assistance?

Bruce Tremore frowned. "I think perhaps at this stage it might be best if our daughter left the room for a while."

"I'm sure my wife will be happy to look after her." Mr. Henderson agreed, and took the child through to the kitchen where his wife was busy baking.

The discussion that followed was awkward to say the least, until the parents found out that the Hendersons had no children of their own. "Not blessed in that way," Mr. Henderson commented.

Jean Tremore delicately suggested that this could be the reason for Mr. Henderson not fully understanding the minds of children.

"Children are after all, very complex little creatures, with vivid imaginations that need no encouraging. Wilma is not yet nine and has obviously been very frightened. Lately she has been having nightmares and I think seeing these vivid pictures, along with unsuitable bible stories, may be the reason."

Mr. Henderson was man enough to admit that perhaps he had put too much emphasis in punishment for wrong-doings. In future he would endeavour to choose more suitable stories for the children and instead, encourage positive thoughts of heavenly rewards for good deeds.

Wilma's parents felt the problem had been satisfactorily resolved, but just as Mr. Henderson stood to bring Wilma back, they heard a ghastly scream. Within seconds the door banged open and Wilma rushed in trembling, her eyes like saucers, gabbling and making no sense whatsoever.

Her mother held her. "Whatever is the matter child?"

Wilma pointed a wobbly finger at her Sunday school teacher, and in a shaky voice said, "He murders things too Mum. He likes looking at dead things, just like in his book." She sobbed. "He's horrible."

"What on earth…" began her father.

They all turned as a red-faced Mrs Henderson entered the room. "I just took her into the study to see your butterfly collection Christopher, and she went crazy. I don't know why."

Her husband shook his head and said. "I think I do; I'm not at all surprised after what I've just been told, not surprised at all. I think I understand more about children's vivid imaginations now. Do you think my dear, that we could all have a cup of tea and something for the child also?"

As his wife bustled off to the kitchen, Mr. Henderson said, "Perhaps now is a good time for us to talk about our misunderstandings, as well as changes to be made at Sunday school." His normally stern face lit up as he smiled at Wilma. "Are we agreed?"

The walk back home in the warmth of the sun was a pleasant one. Wilma skipped along chatting non-stop. She had been so relieved to find out that collecting butterflies was a hobby of many people, and that the small creatures weren't suffering. She also thought Sunday school should be okay now. No more scary books, and happy stories instead would be lovely.

Jean had found Mrs. Henderson (Marion) very pleasant and they had arranged to meet for afternoon tea in the village. They actually had quite a few things in common, including gardening, roses especially, baking and crochet.

Christopher Henderson – 'Do call me Chris,' was interested in learning more about the Rotary organisation to which Bruce Tremore belonged. A really likeable chap once he relaxed, mused Bruce, and a probable new member.

Wilma couched her feelings in words. "I reckon Sundays will now be the best day of the week for all of us." She slipped in between her parents and taking their hands grinned up at them. "Come on Mum, hurry up Dad, I can't wait to tell Maisie the good news."

Her parents looked at each other. Love of each other and Wilma made words unnecessary.

"You run ahead love, your mum and I won't be far behind," her father told her.

He placed his arm around Jean's shoulder. "Lucky, aren't we?"

Jean happily nodded her agreement as holding hands they hurried to reach home.

THE FINAL RETREAT

Lara and Ben had sensibly planned for retirement and both looked forward to the change in lifestyle. Ben had dealt in banking most of his adult life, while Lara worked from home as a magazine writer. This brought in just pin-money as she liked to call it, though she derived a great deal of satisfaction from her efforts. Recalling her dear old Dad's advice, she saved half and spent half. He would have been proud.

One of the things about Lara that Ben really appreciated was the interest and encouragement she had always taken in his work at the bank. There were times when she'd really surprised him with her astute comments. One morning while they'd been having the first cuppa of the day, Ben had mentioned something about an overseas conglomerate take-over and Lara had summed the situation up in a few brief words.

"Not just a pretty face my girl, are you?" he had said to her, ruffling her hair as he passed to get a second cup of tea. Lara had always remembered that.

Due to hard work, their Auckland family home of the last forty odd years was mortgage-free, and they also owned a holiday spot at a beach on the Coromandel Coast. When they'd first bought the bach there had been only four other buildings there. Not so now, with homes of all types and sizes spreading further and further around above the bay. They contrasted from the original humble dwellings to opulent 'look at me' types, standing out like sore thumbs. A blot on the landscape, Lara and Ben reckoned.

They had kept their bach as a comfortable, old-style place, where bunks filled one bedroom and a sofa-bed in the living area was regularly used by visitors. They, as the parents, had the luxury of their own bedroom. When the three children came to stay, tents were often used to cope with the overflow. The bach became a noisy place of competing voices and laughter from which Lara and Ben sometimes escaped. They would walk the length of the beach and occasionally around the point to the next one, welcoming the sea breeze with its sour-sweet salty tang. Or, once they'd bought the boat, they'd head out to the welcome quiet and catch fish for dinner. If the fish were biting, that is!

The bay curved like a horseshoe around the beautifully soft sandy beach. With no tidal rip it provided safe swimming for the children, and the caramel-coloured sand offered easy digging for pipis. A scattering of ancient gnarled pohutukawa trees, shared by both birdlife and humans, provided filtered shade from the sun.

Lara loved to swim, and had always been a little disappointed that Ben didn't share her enthusiasm, even though he was keen on boating. He was happy with his nose in a book, lounging back on a deck chair or out fishing. He was a dab-hand at cooking fish on the barbecue too, which all the family appreciated.

They were still a good-looking couple, even if Ben was losing a bit of greying hair and showed a slightly widened girth. A tall man, he had a commanding presence and a ready smile. Lara too was curvier than years ago, but Ben called it cuddly. Lara quite liked that.

Tall for a woman, she kept her hair coloured a muted brown, though she was becoming more tempted to just relax and let the greys take over; perhaps one day. Lara brought softness into the family, a comfort they all needed at times.

Before they knew it Ben turned sixty-eight and with Lara two years younger, Ben retired. Unplanned, they bought each other a special gift. Lara bought Ben a beautiful waterproof watch and he gave her a choker-length string of the finest cultured pearls.

At the beginning, the thought had been to sell the house, move to the beach and upgrade the bach into a real home. They had talked and talked.

"You know Ben," she told him, "I really would love it if we could keep the bach as a studio. It would be perfect for my writing."

"We could do that," Ben agreed. "And it would be handy to have spare room for any overflow of visitors as well."

So the decision was finally made. A new house would be built towards the front of the land.

A building to blend in with the environment, with solar power of course, to be as off the grid as much as possible. Big windows for the view and sun, covered decks for shade and practical polished concrete floors. There would be just two big bedrooms, though both with en-suites and a sociable, all-in-one cooking, dining and living area. Ben insisted on a separate double garage/workshop, and an oversized carport for the boat.

All was agreed upon and a timeframe put in place. An architect first, then a building permit, a builder -

recommended by friends, and slowly their plans took shape.

An exciting time. Not without frustrations of course, and some minor changes. Finally they were in the new house, their chattels out of storage, and living their dream in their retreat.

Ben found the sandy soil a challenge. The family loved fresh vegetables, so Ben built raised beds which he gradually filled with good soil and compost, adding sheep pellets and blood and bone. He also made a brew from seaweed and fish bones, a bounty from the ocean. The results spoke for themselves and the productive gardens gave Ben an added interest.

Lara decided to keep a diary on day-to-day life at the beach, and from this came the glimmer of an idea of perhaps writing a book. She often met up with people while walking along the shore. Sometimes she stopped to chat and found out all sorts of interesting things, adding these to her diary. She kept the thought of a book to herself; jotted down notes and let the idea take root and grow. Writing really was a solitary occupation and she just loved having her own quiet place in which to write.

Lara would stop and make herself a coffee and sit staring out across the bay, content to watch the ever-changing scene. Boats small and large moored in the bay and with the movements of the sea, rocked like babies to a lullaby. When the tide was full in, Lara found the gentle swishing rhythm of waves breaking up on the sand, music to the soul.

When a boat returned to the boat ramp, you could tell if a load of fish was on-board.

Ravenous seagulls would swoop and dive-bomb the boat, their raucous squawks breaking the serene silence. All to no avail, until finally the gulls left, soaring away to seek their luck elsewhere.

Up on a hill, looking out to sea, a Yacht Club had been built. The commanding position was well chosen being far enough away from the centre of town not to be a disturbance to the local residents. A large well-run restaurant soon proved popular, especially with visiting 'yachties' who moored in the bay for a night or two. A phone call from the beach to the club, and within minutes they would be collected by the cheerful driver in the club's courtesy van. With a ride back guaranteed when they were ready to leave, this service was well patronised.

In the two years since Lara and Ben had become 'permanents' at the beach they had made a few friends, Anne and Ian in particular.

When they had first met them at the Yacht Club, Lara and Ben had considered them a quiet couple. Then over a wine or two, they found just how wrong they were! Anne and Ian were widely travelled and well-read too. They had no children. Not for want of trying it seemed, but they had finally accepted this was not to be. That became the impetus for travel which they enjoyed together. Now retired, Ian enjoyed creating with wood. Not just pine but native rimu and kauri, when he could get it. He spent much of his time in a shed at the back of the property turning out beautiful fruit bowls, candlesticks and platters, amongst other things.

Ian had been 'roped in' as he called it, by the Bay Drama Society. They'd needed a person with his skills to create stage back-drops and props. Why not, he'd decided, and now enjoyed the camaraderie of other volunteers, without whom there would not be a local Drama Society.

Anne was the gardener of the family, so keen to finish her tasks that she could often be seen in an old worn parka working out in the rain. The first time she had done this Ian had shouted to her, "Come inside, you stupid woman, you'll catch your death out there and end up with webbed feet".

This became a well-worn joke but Anne had the last laugh, as her garden grew in fame, eventually attracting bus-loads of garden lovers.

The four friends had a meal together once a month, each taking turns, and in the summer months the men cooked barbecue meals and ladies supplied the salads - easy peasy!

Lara and Ben had been retired now for three years. Three full, busy years. They'd had the occasional trip to Australia and once to the UK, staying with their children and especially, catching up with the grandchildren.

Life had settled into a regular routine. Then the four friends decided to plan a coach and train trip, through both the North and South Island. They each got to choose a special place they wanted to visit, taking their individual interests into account.

Lara's request was simple – specialist bookshops where she could browse for hours. For Ben it had to be boats and fishing. While in Auckland he hoped for a boat trip to Waiheke, and was especially looking forward to the Wellington/Picton crossing and Picton harbour.

Anne would revel in walking the many public parks available, and hopefully, some private gardens that were, like hers, open to the public. Ian was keen on visiting craft markets to get new ideas for his woodturning. Talking to like-minded people he found most rewarding.

They all agreed on two-day stop-overs at Auckland, Rotorua, Christchurch and Queenstown, with three days in Wellington, as one could spend a whole day on just the Te Papa Museum. One-night stops would suffice for the rest. They also concurred on it not being compulsory to eat together every night. Having some time on their own seemed like a good idea.

With the basics sorted, they decided their adventure should be in mid-autumn. Settled weather – hopefully. They envisaged snow-tipped mountains in the South Island, and everywhere, deciduous trees with leaves bowing acknowledgment to the season, rich in every shade of red and gold.

Anne and Ben were elected the ones to plan the trip, check out travel timetables and accommodation, along with recommended places of interest to visit. Anne and Ben being chosen for this task proved a wise move, as Anne in her quiet but firm way acted as a perfect foil to Ben's rather forceful opinions.

Anne's garden retreat was a kitset log cabin. It nestled close to the backdrop of pines she had planted some years ago. Sometimes she figured all it needed was snow, then it could have been a scene from the Canadian Rockies. Rather a laugh really, being at the beach. She loved her quaint hideaway complete with covered deck and wide opening doors.

It was here that she planned changes and additions to her garden according to her whims, and the forces of the seasons. One complete wall held bookshelves full of gardening books, well-worn from regular use; obviously not always with clean fingers!

The cabin became the ideal place for Anne and Ben to study travel brochures, and search the internet for the latest information on each of the proposed stop-overs. There were regular coffee breaks, and both found themselves surprised at the differences they discovered in each other. Pleasantly so, as without even noticing, each of them revealed a little more of themselves. Laughter came easily and often as they planned the trip, agreeing more often than not, surprisingly. Of course they still had to check with Lara and Ian for their opinions as well.

There never seemed enough hours in the day. So much for a leisurely retirement. But really, both couples thrived on keeping busy.

Even after the travel plans were approved and the trip booked, Ben sometimes popped in for a coffee, and when Anne was away for a few days he was surprised to find himself at a bit of a loose end. Perhaps that should have been the time to acknowledge the warning signs, for they were definitely there. The way Anne's face lit up when he put his head in the door of her hide-away. His pleasure at just watching her and listening to her quietly expressed but interesting thoughts.

At home, Lara became aware of Ben being somehow different.

Nothing she could put her finger on, but almost as if he was becoming vague – not listening to her, and at times seeming miles away. She even wondered if it was the beginning of ageing – but of course it couldn't be; could it? Anyway, she was spending more time in her studio, having finally started writing what, she hoped, may eventually become a book. She pushed her fleeting concerns about Ben from her mind.

Ian was more often than not working away in his shed, skilfully crafting his beautiful wooden pieces, or down at the Drama Society's little theatre. As far as he was concerned, nothing had changed in his and Anne's comfortable world.

Summer came with a vengeance. Not only searing temperatures but hot sticky humidity that defied sleep. When rain did arrive it wasn't for long, and resulted in even higher humidity. Thank goodness for the beach and the cooling sea.

After breakfast one morning Lara tidied up and as usual said, "I'd better get on with my writing I suppose," adding, "What are your plans for the morning Ben?"

Without looking up from reading the morning paper Ben replied, "I might get in a bit of fishing, so I'll take something to eat with me just in case. Don't know how long I'll be, depends on whether the fish are biting or not."

"Okay love," Lara acknowledged. "See you later. Take care." And off she went.

Absorbed in her writing, Lara stopped and stretched to ease her back. She was amazed to note the time on her laptop showed twelve noon. Her mind wandered back to Ben and his rather odd ways of late. One really concerning thing was their sex life, or rather the lack of it! Ben was always tired these days. He read in bed, then turning off his lamp, said a quick goodnight. Not even a cuddle. Then the drone of snoring would begin. It hadn't been like that before. Lara even tried buying a couple of rather sexy nighties, but she may as well have not bothered for all the reaction they caused. Cooking his favourite meals and serving up candle-lit dinners also proved a waste of time. What else could she do? Vitamins. Vitamins for men. She'd seen them at the supermarket. Perhaps he needed those.

"What on earth have you got these for?" was Ben's reaction when she first produced them. "We eat well, I don't need any bloody vitamins."

Lara sat scanning the last couple of pages and one part just didn't seem right. How to improve on it? Her head and neck ached a little, and checking the time again she decided to take a break, and returned to the house for a bite of lunch.

As she ate, Lara kept thinking of Ben and odd things she recalled. The last couple of times he'd been out fishing he'd come back empty handed. That was most unusual for him. And he didn't have much to say these days. Not like him at all. She wondered, was he feeling neglected with her spending so much time writing? Could that be the problem?

Then, in her mind's eye, she saw Ben laughing at something Anne had said the other day. The look on Anne's face. Ben's face flushing. Suddenly, she was questioning everything, had she been stupid, had she been naïve? Surely it couldn't be, not her Ben and Anne, no way.

But could they possibly be having an affair? This might explained why Anne was so tied up of late, not even having time for their usual catch-up weekly lunch. If her guess was right, it was no wonder Anne avoided her.

Writing was the last thing on her mind now. Lara needed a good long walk, time to think, to make sense of her thoughts. Slipping on her old beach sneakers and grabbing a sunhat, she left the house.

At their end of the beach there wasn't a soul to be seen. Not unusual during weekdays, unlike weekends when hordes of weekenders arrived. Lara gazed out to sea. No sign of Ben coming back yet. Normally she would worry a little if he was out too long, but not today. She still hoped that all she had been thinking was totally wrong.

After about twenty minutes, Lara reached the end of the bay and sat on a rock to catch her breath. She removed her hat, letting the gentle breeze ruffle her hair, and breathed in deeply. Her head and neck felt a bit better and after a few minutes she carried on, clambering up onto the rocks that led to the next small bay. The tide was on its way out, so she knew she had plenty of time to return the same way. She noted the jagged edges of oysters now uncovered by the receding tide. What a mess they would make of you if you fell. She walked warily.

Reaching the final point between the two bays, she stayed close to the overhanging cliffs, glad of the sheltering shade of the scarlet laden pohutukawa trees. That was when she spotted the boat. Not just any boat, but their boat; hers and Ben's. Even without the bright blue name 'NEPTUNE' Lara would have recognised their boat.

She stared, but could not see a sign of Ben. Of course, he'd probably gone up into the bush for a 'Mother Nature' visit. Suddenly, from around the other side of the boat he appeared, swimming for God's sake. Ben swimming! What the…?

Lara was just about to call to him when she saw he was not alone. Another swimmer followed. Lara could only make out a fair head and a small body, but she instinctively knew who it would be. Ben turned and dived at the other person. They both disappeared briefly beneath the waves and then re-appeared nearer the beach. As they stood up in the shallow water, Lara's fears were confirmed.

Anne stood there, shaking water from her hair, and laughing up at Ben, punched him playfully.

Lara, her hand held to her mouth, could not have moved if she'd wanted to. Pressed hard against the cliff, she watched, horrified.

The tableau played out. Ben and Anne grasped each other and kissed deeply, hands sliding over and around each other's bare, water slicked bodies. They stopped and stood just gazing at each other. Then, as if in silent agreement, they grasped hands and ran up towards the grassy mounds, disappearing from view.

Lara felt sick and dropped to her knees heedless of the sharp encrusted rocks. She didn't remember walking home but there she was, in the bathroom. Shaking all over and vomiting her lunch down the toilet.

She had this awful grinding pain in her chest and as she stood up she saw blood trickling down her legs onto her bare feet. She must have taken her sneakers off when she got home, but she couldn't recall doing so.

If only that was all it was. Cuts and bruises. If only.

The sight of Ben and Anne replayed itself in her mind. She knew what the next scene would have been. At the thought, waves of nausea washed over her again. Then anger cut in. "Damn them. Damn and blast them both to hell!" she shouted.

Her Ben, how could he? And Anne. How could she do this to Ian? Both of them betrayed. All those years with Ben wrecked, obviously meaningless to him. The same questions went over and over in her mind. How could Ben do this? At his age. And why?

Hate consumed Lara like a roaring hot flame. Hurt, she would hurt him too. Let him feel her pain.

She went to their bedroom and took out the special box that contained his treasured gift. The pearls. Sitting on the bed, their bed, she sat rolling their satin smoothness between her fingers. Like you would a rosary, she imagined. But no prayers were being offered up. Why pray when there was nothing left? Her marriage to Ben was over.

Very calmly, Lara took the pearls through to the kitchen and picked up the kitchen scissors. She sat on the deck and looked out at the beckoning sea. She knew it would be cool and comforting.

Unlike Ben, and at the memory this brought back she grimaced, she had always loved swimming.

As she walked slowly along the pathway and down towards the water's edge, Lara cut one pearl for Ben, one pearl for Anne. Over and over she repeated the mantra, dropping pearl after pearl to lie shimmering beneath the golden sun.

She reached the glistening sea and let the scissors fall from her fingers onto the sand. The pearls, like her marriage, all gone.

Above, a lone seagull cried as it wheeled and rose high with the wind to look down on the deserted beach.

Lara sat back luxuriating in the comfort that only business class flight can bring. She began to smile; just a little. She envisaged the scene at the 'Retreat'. Blood splotches in the bathroom and the bedroom, leading right through the house and onto the deck. The cut-off pearls and the scissors close to the water's edge. Panic, she hoped, horror and guilt. Police and questions. Ben suffering.

Lara patted her large hold-all. Travelling light she had taken only her precious laptop and the new bag, used for the first time. No one would know it was missing.

Dear old Ian, tough for him too. A phone call from her mobile was all it had taken for Ian to collect her and drive her to the nearest airport, offering his farewells and a promise to remain silent. Lara felt so sorry for him, his life also in tatters.

Lara had all she needed. Her astute investments, lessons learned from her banker husband, had over the years done extremely well. Confirmation of Ben's comment all those years ago that 'she was *not* just a pretty face.' Her villa on the French Riviera in the southeast of France awaited her arrival.

Yes, it would be a difficult time for her children, and this was the only thing she felt guilty about, but she would contact them before too long. Just long enough for Ben to suffer, to feel her pain.

Lara looked up at the hostess and with a "thank you," she accepted the proffered champagne. A sip confirmed it was exquisite, absolutely exquisite. She held up the glass and quietly murmured a toast. To a new life.

Vive La France!

POETIC JUSTICE

The elderly gentleman drove his spotless dark green Suzuki Swift slowly and carefully, around and around the supermarket carpark, looking for a free space. He was in luck, and waited patiently as a lady backed out. He swung in to the gap, wary of the room he had left on each side of the car. Getting out he again checked his line-up to see it was perfect.

You could tell by the way he moved from the car that age had taken its toll, though as he walked into the store and straightened up, he visibly dropped a few years. A casual observer would have thought his bearing military, and they wouldn't be wrong. He was ex-Army, NZ Army actually, from World War II. Perhaps this was why every morning he still showered and shaved the old-fashioned way; no electric razor for him. He never went out without wearing a clean, pressed shirt and checking his shoes were shined till they gleamed. Old habits but good habits, he believed.

Once in the store he stood to check his shopping list before choosing a trolley. One that didn't wobble or prove stubborn to operate. If he ran the store, trollies would be checked regularly and defective ones repaired or thrown out.

"Morning Mr. Parsons," came a female voice from the corner. "And how are we this morning?" The matronly grey-haired woman sitting at a raffle table smiled at him.

"Well, I wouldn't presume to know how you feel, Mrs Thurston, but as for myself, I am very well, thank you."

He was not so deaf that he couldn't hear the woman's muttered reply to her raffle companion. "Silly old man." But he felt it too trivial to bother about. Regardless of her rude comment he would buy raffle tickets as he left the store. The St. Johns Ambulance Society needed all the help they could get. In his opinion it was disgraceful that the government didn't fully fund this marvellous public service.

Wielding his trolley defensively, he entered the fray, for that was how he felt about shopping. A necessary chore; the sooner over and done with the better. Right, vegetables first. As Jim Parsons looked at the vegies and the prices, he was glad that he grew much of these himself. Fresher too, by the look of some of the produce! Still, there were always some items out-of-season in NZ, such as grapes, and at this time of year, apples and oranges too. All needed to make up a fruit salad, enough to last him a few days.

As Jim put the last of the fruit and vegies in his trolley, he couldn't help but notice the lad ahead of him. Scruffy jeans – that seemed to be common these days, as was the hood that hung down from the jacket he wore. Hoodies, he'd heard them called. The young ones seemed to wear them even in the hottest of weather – why, was beyond his comprehension. The lad's dirty sneakers and greasy hair that needed a cut made him shudder. Should bring back Army conscription, he thought. Teach these young kids a bit of pride in their appearance. Hard work and plenty of it never hurt anyone; his generation knew that.

He watched as the lad lifted and sniffed at some fruit, then put it back down. What an odd thing to do, he thought. Jim checked his list. Yes, cheese next. Blue vein and a good tasty cheese for cooking. He thought back to when his dear wife Valerie was alive. She used to call the blue vein 'stinky cheese', and he smiled at the memory. Now butter – proper butter, not one messed about with additives and certainly *not* margarine.

"Hello Jim." A voice came from behind him. "I thought it was you."

Jim turned around. "Hello Colin, haven't seen you for ages. How's life treating you? Still playing bowls are you?"

The two men chatted for a few minutes. "Better get on I suppose." Colin said. "Mary's waiting in the car. I just popped in for a bottle of wine to take with us to the daughter's. Having dinner with them tonight. Well, take care of yourself Jim, see you later."

Jim acknowledged the farewell and looked back at his list. Now, where was I, he pondered. Oh, yes. The meat department next. Prime beef mince, always a good standby, a packet of sausages, and if on special, a steak or two. This done, he stopped at the frozen section and picked up a good deal on a chicken and a steak-and-kidney pie. An economical shopper, he expected to get three meals out of the chicken and two meals from the pie.

He paused again, what next? Ah yes, chocolate biscuits and a packet of Werthers to satisfy his sweet tooth. One has to have some pleasures in life. He headed down what it amused him to think of as, 'the aisle of temptation'.

There was that strange young boy again. What on earth is he doing now? Jim wondered. He looks decidedly shifty; looking around him as if…

Good God, he has! The blighter's slipped a bar of chocolate into his jacket pocket. Jim looked around. None of the other shoppers seemed to have noticed. Any thought of further shopping went right out of his head.

The boy seemed to be going towards the checkout and Jim followed close behind.

There were a couple of people at each checkout and Jim watched the boy hesitate. The female supervisor had just approved the wine purchase of the customer being served. She seemed to stare at the boy for an overly long time. Jim felt sick in the stomach at what might happen to the boy next. He had to do something, but what?

Tapping the lad on the shoulder he said, "Hey Brian, I nearly forgot that bar of chocolate I gave you. Better put it in the trolley or you'll have me done for stealing." The old man chuckled. "Imagine going to prison at my age. Mind you, the meals there might be better than my cooking!" The checkout girl and the supervisor laughed at his comment.

The lad took the chocolate bar and placed it in the trolley with a muttered, "Sorry about that."

It was now Jim's turn at the checkout and he asked the lad, "Give me a hand with these would you Brian?" Finally, with the groceries paid for, they went towards the exit.

"Oh, there you are Mr. Parsons," shrilled Mrs. Thurston as soon as she spotted him. "Shopping all done? Got a helper have you?"

"Yes, to both questions Mrs Thurston. Is it the usual three tickets for five dollars?" Mrs Thurston nodded in agreement. "Right, three tickets it is, thank you."

Jim paid for the raffle tickets. "I reckon between us we can carry these few bags to the car Brian," he said, and pushed the trolley into the bay provided. As the boy helped, he bumped into the old man. "Sorry," he muttered.

Out in the carpark he turned to Jim. "Thanks for getting me out of the crap in there. Dumb thing to do I suppose."

"It certainly was," Jim agreed. "Really dumb."

As they began to load the bags into the car-boot, Jim wobbled a bit on his feet and clutched at the side of the car.

The boy grabbed his arm. "You okay, old man?"

Jim shook his head as if to clear it. "Sure, it's just a little dizzy spell. Happens sometimes, it'll pass. Low blood pressure the Doc says. Nothing serious though. Well, thanks for the hand lad, and don't go nicking anything more from stores. A mug's game, that is."

With a grunt and a casual wave the lad took off, hood up and shoulders hunched against the breeze, heading away from the carpark. As Jim drove out he saw the boy disappear down a nearby alleyway.

In another street, the lad that Jim had called Brian, reached a rather battered Ford Cortina. He opened the passenger door and clambered in.

A slightly older but similar-looking youth sat in the driving seat. "What the hell's taken ya so long?" he asked. "I was beginning to think you'd got nicked. Did ya get a hit?"

"Of course," smirked 'Brian', "Do you think I'm dumb or something?"

"Well let's have it then. Let's see how good your pick was today, Tosh." He reached out his hand.

Tosh slipped his hand into the pocket of his hoodie. "What, where?" He checked his other pockets. "Shit, I don't believe it. He's bloody well done me over. The old bastard's played me. Dizzy spell be damned. The cunning old bugger."

Driving along the busy highway, Jim Parsons sat back enjoying his favourite CD of Doris Day. Smiling, he envisaged the scene when the young thief found he'd been tricked at his own game. He hoped the lad had learned a lesson, but sadly, he didn't think so.

Jim's wallet sat snugly in his back pocket, just where it belonged.

He had enjoyed his years in the Secret Service Division of the New Zealand Army. Especially the latter years based in England; where he had become a personal trainer. He was rather pleased that he hadn't lost his smooth touch. He still recalled 'use your brain, remain calm. Distract and make your move'. Just like today. And Mrs Thurston had called him an old fool?

There is a saying, 'There's no fool like an old fool.' Today Jim was happy to have proved that he certainly wasn't an old fool.

He glanced up at the clear blue sky and thought, 'You'd be proud of me, wouldn't you Valerie my sweet?'

He felt the warmth of her love still, and contented, he concentrated on reaching home.

IF ONLY

The 1970s were times of change in New Zealand. Jobs weren't as easy to come by and high oil prices had hit the country hard. More imported goods saw a decline in 'New Zealand made'. Colour television had arrived, along with the fad of fondue dinner parties. Fashion was challenging, from flared trousers for men, to jumpsuits for women. Rock and Roll continued in popularity and in 1977 the death of Elvis Presley made headlines. Of growing concern to many New Zealanders was the nuclear testing in the Pacific.

The influx of English immigrants during the sixties had eased. These were hardworking folk, now with New Zealand-born children growing up well and happy. When they first arrived, some had been unhappy with their lot. Fortunately, those who moaned about what they saw as a lack of the comforts of 'home' were in the minority. Even some of the folk who came from England were ashamed of those who whinged. The majority made new friends and settled in well.

One such friendship began as Janine sat with her little boy Josh, waiting for a bus to her nearest shopping centre, Highbury. A tall, very young woman with a mass of curly blonde hair arrived. She was noticeably pregnant; her fair skinned face flushed in the heat. She smiled tentatively, glad to sit down. The young woman spoke nicely to Josh and by the time they got off the bus in Highbury, Janine knew a lot about her.

Milly and her husband Phil were English; newly arrived in the country and she was not yet seventeen. With her parents' consent she and Phil had married when she was only sixteen so they could emigrate to New Zealand. Here Phil had a job waiting him at the Glenbrooke steel mill. Milly was amazed at the space, living surrounded by lush farmland and everything so fresh and green, with trees, parks and beaches all close by. Just wonderful, she told Janine, her eyes shining.

Then Milly looked wistful. "I do really miss my family though, especially my mum and dad." Her eyes welled up. Janine made up her mind to invite her for a cup of tea or coffee, and so began a new friendship. Janine admired Milly for making the break from family and home at such a young age.

Milly said that if they had stayed in the UK they would have rented a council flat – no green grass there – and perhaps eventually upgraded to renting a terraced house. Most people, according to Milly, rented all their lives. Like her and Phil's own parents did and they thought themselves very comfortable in their semi-detached two-storied house. Of course there was also the well-to-do. Class structure Milly called it, and was glad it wasn't in New Zealand!

There were some things they'd have to get used to, though. Ice-cold beer for one, and rugby being the national sport, not soccer! Milly of course missed friends and family, but Phil had made a couple of friends at work and enjoyed their laid-back ways.

Milly confessed that she had found the Christmas just gone to be quite strange with hot weather, not cold. No snow and no carol singers knocking on the door on Christmas Eve. Recently some neighbours had invited them over for a barbecue, which was a lot of fun, and later everyone went to the beach. Swimming and picnicking on leftovers. All-in-all, she found life in this country wonderful.

In recent times, many women had begun going back to work as soon as the last of their children started school, especially those who needed the extra income. Janine planned to do the same. In the meantime there were three close neighbours with whom she and the children shared times at the nearby beach, and special occasions like children's birthday parties. It was always good to be able to talk over problems, whether about the children or your marriage. Out of the four of them, only one actually had a car of her own, but over the next few years this was to become more common.

Milly was welcomed into this group and the women laughingly called themselves the Fabulous Five. Over the years they shared many different interests, as well as friendship.

One day, when walking to the local shops, Janine met a newly-arrived neighbour. Gloria was in an older age group; probably mid-forties. Must have been, as she and her husband Mike had two adult daughters who had already left home.

Gloria was slender and immaculately dressed, her blonde hair swept up and pinned with a tortoiseshell clip. Gold earrings, bracelet and necklace gleamed. Over time, Janine noticed that Gloria was never seen without makeup, jewellery or her fingernails beautifully manicured.

Gloria worked part-time at an up-market Art Gallery in Auckland's CBD. Her real love though was being part of the Drama Society that met and performed plays at the old Takapuna Pump House. To Janine, this explained her elegant bearing, outgoing confidence and beautiful diction.

Because of the age difference and interests between the Fabulous Five and Gloria, she didn't join in with the group. She did however enjoy sharing an occasional coffee with Janine.

Gloria and her husband Mike had been living in Birkdale about a year, when one morning, Gloria arrived unexpectedly. "I'm sorry Janine," she said, "But I have to talk to someone, and I certainly can't talk to my daughters about this. Can I come in?"

"Of course you can," Janine said. "I'll put the jug on and we'll have a coffee."

They sat at the table and Gloria took a deep breath. "Mike has been having an affair. For a long time actually. Last night he told me he's moving out, going to shack-up with her I suppose." She smiled bitterly then burst into tears.

Janine sat stunned, lost for words. She did her best to comfort Gloria and gradually she quietened down. Gloria had accepted the marriage was over. She'd been battling to keep their marriage intact for so long that in one way she was relieved now that the struggle was over. Though Gloria called it conscience money, Mike was signing the house over to her. With his thriving legal practice, he could well afford it and in that respect Gloria knew she was lucky.

To stop herself dwelling on being dumped, Gloria increased her work hours to full-time, and over the next few months Janine rarely saw her. Then it became obvious that Gloria had a man-friend. More than a friend, Janine's husband Ray commented, as he did stay overnight.

"Well, that's her business I reckon," Janine said. "As long as she's happy, that's the main thing."

Janine was in the front garden dead-heading roses one day, when she met Gloria's new friend for the first time. On their way to the corner dairy, Gloria stopped and introduced Stefan. Janine was surprised to note their considerable age difference. She guessed Stefan to be in his late twenties, thirty at most. A natty – if slightly poncy – dresser, he was tall, swarthy and lean, with collar-length dark hair. A small pointed beard put the finishing touch to his rather Latin appearance. As he looked at Janine she felt uncomfortable, and afterwards, wondered why. Had it been his tawny eyes, or the intense way he had looked at her? She had shaken the feeling off as daft, but had been glad to see him go.

Janine and Gloria got together for a coffee one morning, the first time for ages. Janine learned that Gloria had met Stefan at a Drama Society meeting at the Takapuna Pump House. They had been looking for new members and Stefan was interested. He turned out to be quite a good actor, having a very good memory for lines. He worked erratic hours as a barman, helping friends out whenever they were short-staffed. As he didn't like being tied down, that suited him fine. Never been married and liked it that way, he'd told Gloria.

It was a couple months later, while walking home from the dairy, that Janine met Gloria. As she came closer Janine noticed her odd walk, unsteady somehow. Then she noticed Gloria wasn't dressed in her usual immaculate manner. Her clothes were rumpled, and ye gods! She was wearing her gardening shoes.

Janine greeted her. "Ages since I saw you Gloria. How are you?"

"Okay I guess. Been very busy lately. Sorry, I can't stop to chat, I'm off to the butcher's. Stefan likes his steak. See you later Janine."

They went their separate ways, and as Janine walked home she wondered, was it her imagination, or had that been a bruise on Gloria's right cheekbone? Hard to tell under all that makeup. But Gloria certainly hadn't been her normal chatty self.

That night when Ray got home from work, Janine told him about the meeting. "I saw Gloria today when I went to the dairy. Haven't seen her for ages. She didn't look at all well. Looked really scruffy. She'd even gone out in her gardening shoes!"

Ray looked at her. "Gloria, scruffy? That's hard to believe."

"Well she was, and not only that, she sort-of walked funny."

"You're probably imagining things Jan."

"I'm not you know, but never mind." Janine shrugged, and got on with dishing up dinner.

One Saturday morning as Janine was hanging out the washing, she jumped with fright hearing what seemed like pistol shots. She walked further down the back garden and looked across to where the sound came from. It wasn't pistol shots.

Cr-rack, cr-rack cr-rack. Stefan was the culprit. She could see him on the back lawn at Gloria's house.

He stood with legs wide apart, swinging a long black leather whip in the air, and with every downward flick the same violent sound rent the air.

Josh came running to see what was going on. "Look at him Mum, he's got to be mad."

"I agree love," Janine told her son. "That man is definitely strange."

A few weeks later Janine was taking the mail from the letterbox when Gloria came walking down the road. This time there was no mistaking what she saw. Both sides of Gloria's face were badly bruised, her bottom lip split and swollen. No amount of makeup could hide the damage. Janine took her arm and gently said, "Come on in for a cup of coffee Gloria."

She was surprised how docilely Gloria followed her indoors. In an automatic reaction to being inside Gloria removed her sunglasses. Janine was horrified at what she saw. The area around her eyes showed a dark blotchy purple and both eyes were swollen and totally bloodshot with not a sign of white to be seen. Janine felt ill. Gloria had been badly beaten, and Janine could imagine who was responsible.

As if a dam had broken, Gloria's words gushed forth. Janine sat and listened.

"It was Stefan. He gets very angry when he drinks, and that's most nights. He says I'm an incompetent idiot, I can't get anything right. I'm a lousy cook, and useless actor. I'm old and haggard and sex with me no longer interests him. Except after he beats me. I don't know why, but he always wants me then. He says I'm going mad, and maybe I am. I just can't seem to think straight these days."

"I'm going to ring the police. Get them to come here and talk to you. You have to lay a formal complaint. The bastard needs to be put away for what he's done to you."

Gloria looked horrified. "I can't do that. It's just the drink that does it. Stefan is really lovely when he's not drinking." Tears ran down her face as she sobbed, "He even buys me flowers."

Janine ignored this. "At least let's get you to your doctor. You can talk to him, and your eyes are such a mess. I'll ring and see if you can get to see him straight away."

Standing up, Gloria shook her head. "No. I don't want that either. I have to go home."

Nothing Janine said could persuade her. Sadly, she watched Gloria walk away, back to – only God knew what.

That night she told Ray what had happened. He shrugged.

"Don't get involved Jan. You may not know the whole story and anyway, what happens between couples is their own private business. You won't get thanked for sticking your nose in. Best you keep out of it."

Janine didn't see Gloria for at least two weeks. She phoned her a couple of times but there was no reply.

Then one weekend Josh came rushing indoors saying, "Mum, there's an ambulance at the weird man's house." Of course he meant Gloria's. Janine hurried along there, but too late. The ambulance was vanishing in the distance, with Stefan's car following close behind.

For a couple of days there was no sign of anyone at Gloria's, and it was with relief that Janine saw Gloria's daughters arrive. Anxious to find out what had happened to her friend, Janine hurried along to the house. Was Gloria all right? Was she still in hospital and if so, which one? All questions she wanted to ask. The girls seemed pleased to see her and invited her in.

Janine looked at their red and puffy eyes and knew something awful had happened. After Janine sat down, Tina explained.

"Mum had a fall, here in the lounge." She gestured towards the tiled fire surround. "She hit her head there. Well, that's what Stefan told the ambulance guys. Not the first time she'd had a fall, according to him." She choked up and had to stop.

Maria continued, "I'm sorry Janine, but she died in the ambulance before it arrived at the hospital. Tina and I, we didn't even get to see her, talk to her, before… to say goodbye."

Janine looked away as they cried and wanted to weep too.

"Did you know she was drinking of late?" Maria asked. "We could smell it on her. Seemed odd. You know, Mum hardly ever drank alcohol when she was married to Dad."

Tina added, "That Stefan, he would drive anyone to drink. I couldn't stand the creep. Mum wasn't happy lately, I'm sure of that."

Janine sat still, her mind in a whirl. Should she say anything? Would it help, or would it just cause more hurt and problems? And what did she really know? She murmured sympathetic words adding, "Do let me know if there is anything I can do to help." Tears welling, she said her goodbyes and fled for home.

Ray arrived home to find a very upset wife. Janine told him of her visit to Gloria's, and that Gloria had died and the awful way it had happened.

"I should have done more, Ray. I should have gone to the police myself. She might still be alive. And what if he hit her, knocked her down? If he did, he's a murderer. And he gets away with it."

"You're getting carried away Jan," Ray insisted. "You don't know anything for sure. Gloria wouldn't have spoken out against him, you know that. You said she seemed unsteady on her feet one day when you met her. Well, she may have been drinking that morning and taken a tumble. It's very sad, but we'll never know. You'll just have to accept that."

Janine went to Gloria's funeral and shed tears for such a waste of a life. As she knelt in the church she swore that if ever she knew of cruelty to anyone, ever again, she would speak out – regardless of the consequences.

Stefan had seemingly vanished, and thank heavens for that Janine thought. Probably looking for another gullible woman. She hoped she never saw him again.

Gloria's death became the catalyst for Janine's involvement in the organisation 'Shine.' For many years she helped families, not just women, become safe, grow strong and often, begin new lives. This was her personal atonement for, as she saw it, not speaking out when she should have, and doing more for Gloria.

Perhaps she could have made a difference. She would never know, but there were still times when she thought, 'if only!'

A HELPING HAND

The store hummed with the noise of piped music and people in the frenzied count-down to Christmas. Brightly coloured signs everywhere displayed bargains to be had, exhorting everyone to buy, buy. Instant happiness guaranteed!

Among the crowd, a man in his mid-sixties stood still, his forehead puckered in a deep frown as he stared down at his shopping list. If you had to describe him, you would say he was an ordinary looking man except for the coarse dark eyebrows that spread like uplifted wings above deep-set eyes.

A hassled young mother passed, the child in her firm grip knocking into the man. "Watch what you're doing Simon. Sorry," she muttered to the man, not waiting for an answer as she hurried on.

Poor little beggar, the man thought, so much for the Christmas spirit! Reading the aisle signs he headed towards 'Bathroom Linen'. Towels, that's the ticket. Lisa used to say you can never have enough towels. Three sets, one for each of the girls, good, I can cross that off.

Now for the grandkids, let's see. Yes, vouchers from the Toy Warehouse, can't go wrong there and vouchers for the guys too – from Bunnings or Placemakers, either would do.

Also on the list was the Pavlova he had promised Jane he'd bring to the Christmas dinner, and as usual, a bottle of her favourite wine – Wither Hills Chardonnay.

On his way to the checkout he spotted the display of tinned biscuits. Blimey, he thought, I nearly forgot Isobel. His neighbour was a dear old soul who took in his mail for him when he was away and kept an eagle eye on the place. Isobel didn't miss a beat, even if she was going on ninety. He chose her favourites, Campbell's Shortbread, adding these to the basket.

With the first lot of his shopping done, he left the store and headed for his car.

"Hey, Colin."

Colin turned to see John, a friend from the Bowling Club approaching, hand extended.

"Compliments of the Season," John said, as they shook hands. "How are you, and what are you up to on Christmas day?"

Eventually, promising to get together for a beer after the Christmas rush was over, the men went their separate ways.

On the way home, Colin stopped off at Bunnings to buy vegie plants and a bag of sheep pellets, also getting the vouchers needed for the menfolk. He didn't send Christmas cards, just rang the people he considered most important.

Driving home, he mulled over the way Lisa would have reacted to his not sending cards and not buying just the right gifts for each and every one of the family. But women, he reckoned, had the art of Christmas shopping perfected, men just didn't!

Back home Colin put the jug on for a coffee and set about making his lunch. He glanced out the window at the row of Iceberg roses Lisa had planted.

Three years, and he still missed her like hell; still felt lonely. There had been no warning. Right out of the blue it had come, heart, the Doc said. And she was the energetic one, always coercing him to eat better and exercise more. You just never know.

It was the quiet that got to him the most. Lisa had seldom been quiet. Bit of a chatter box really, and now… He'd thought of getting another animal. It was a few years since they'd had a dog; and a cat. Maybe a cat would be nice – company anyway.

Just as he sat down with his lunch the phone rang. He held the phone away from his ear as his mate's voice boomed down the line.

"Hi Bob," he replied. "That's very nice of you and Trish, but I'm going to Jane and Tom's for Christmas dinner. Thanks all the same. Yes, a barbecue a few days later would be very nice. Okay if I call you? And a very Happy Christmas to you and Trish too."

Friends, he thought, good friends. Jolly nice of them.

The next morning dawned bright and clear. Good, after breakfast he would get in the new vegie plants, then he must pop over to Isobel's and let her know he would be away over Christmas.

As usual Colin went down the drive to collect the morning's Herald. Though why I bother I don't know, he pondered. First page will be either Donald bloody Trump or house prices in Auckland–take your pick!

Breakfast over and the house tidied up, he spent an hour or so in the garden. Looking up at the cloudless sky prompted him to give the whole garden a good soaking before going back indoors.

Having showered and dressed tidily, he went over to see Isobel. She welcomed him in with her usual chirpy, "Don't worry about taking your shoes off Colin, come on in." Her eyes lit up as she spotted the tin of shortbread.

As Colin handed it to her she said, "My favourites, as you well know. How kind you are, almost a tradition now isn't it?"

Then in answer to Colin's request, "Of course I'll keep an eye on the place for you. Now, have you got time for a cuppa?"

"Yes, that would be nice. Thanks Isobel." They sat at the dining table and chatted. Colin asked, "Isobel, do you know of a place where they have cats needing a home?"

"Well, let me think; yes, I know, there's that place at Te Amangi. I've heard it's run by a woman, gather she just asks for a donation to cover her costs. Mary Moss got a cat from her a couple of years ago, lovely big ginger moggy it is and great company for her."

"Sounds just the job. I'll go and see the place, see what I think. Thanks Isobel, and thanks for the cuppa. Better go and get my washing on next, always something to do."

As he walked back home, Colin noted the shrubs that needed trimming and then decided no, they could wait. He'd get the washing out then go for a drive and find that place Isobel had told him about - the Cat lady.

It took Colin about forty minutes driving to get to Te Amangi. He'd had to stop and ask a local farmer if he was on the right road, before finally arriving at what had to be the correct place. The sign could easily have been missed as it hung cockeyed on the post at one side of a driveway.

'Patsy's Cats' it stated. A second sign read 'Free Range Eggs for Sale.' Could do with some of those, he thought.

Colin looked at the rutted driveway, but reckoned at least with it being dry he wouldn't get bogged down. Here we go, he said to himself, nothing ventured, nothing gained, and steered the car into the driveway. No sign or sound of cats so far!

Flipping heck, the drive went on and on. On one side a gentle slope swept down to a slow trickling stream and on the high side, tall pine trees created shade. Colin was beginning to think he'd come to the wrong place when finally, rounding another sharp curve, he came to an abrupt end. The drive was now blocked by a farm-gate.

Getting out of the car Colin checked the gate and was relieved to find the padlock was hanging open. Further on there was a rather scruffy house and down near a grove of citrus trees, a group of buildings was scattered spasmodically. Not a soul to be seen. He made sure to close the gate after him.

As he walked toward the house he spotted a woman, bent over an old concrete horse trough. Holding on to the trough with one hand, she seemed to be scrubbing like mad. Without thinking, he admired the way her jeans fitted her tight round bottom. He was shocked at himself, what the hell had got into him? He hadn't thought that way for years. Coughing loudly he asked, "I guess you're the cat lady?"

The woman swung around and straightened up. A grin spread across an impish face and eyes of the most intense blue looked him up and down.

"Well," she said, hands indicating the space around them. "There's no one else here, is there?"

Colin deliberately took his time glancing around as if to check. "Sure doesn't look like it." He grinned. "In that case, you must be Patsy. I'm Colin and I think I need a cat."

"Yes, I'm Patsy, but right now what *I* need is a cold drink." She wiped her forehead with a not-too-clean piece of rag. "Follow me."

Colin stood at the doorway and watched her as she took a large glass jar from an ancient fridge and unscrewed the lid. He pondered on her age. Hard to tell, could be anything from late fifties to early sixties.

She tilted her head in question. "Home-made ginger beer?"

"Great, that'd be great," Colin replied. "Could we sit out here on the veranda? Looks nice and cool."

"Good idea, then we can talk about cats."

They sat quietly for a few minutes and then both started talking at the same time. Laughing, Patsy said, "You go first. To start with, tell me why you want a cat."

That set Colin back for a bit, but he decided to be straight up with her. He stared into the distance.

"My wife Lisa died just over three years ago and the house is too quiet and I need company. We used to have animals. Our cat was a beaut, he'd sit on my lap of an evening and followed my wife around the garden in the daytime. Lisa was a keen gardener."

He finally looked at Patsy who saw the sadness in his eyes. "Thank you for telling me. I'm sorry for your loss, but I think I understand." After a quiet few minutes she said, "Now Colin, if you've finished your drink we can go and see if I might have the right cat for you. Or rather which cat might decide to choose you! They do that sometimes you know. Do you have a preference, male or female?"

"Either or, makes no difference to me."

"Come on then," Patsy said, and led the way down to the out-buildings. Looking at the state of them Colin commented, "I reckon your husband has plenty to keep him busy."

Patsy laughed. "Some chance of that seeing as I've never been married. Got close to it a couple of times when I was young, but somehow it never seemed quite right, or maybe I just got cold feet. Anyway, I'm happy enough here, even though I really could do with a man's helping hand at times. These buildings for example, the cats' sleeping quarters really should be lined. It gets darned cold here come winter."

Nearing the building, Colin could now hear cats loudly demanding attention.

"They know my voice," Patsy explained. "They're normally quiet except at feed-times."

Colin followed her into a secure area and then through another door into the cattery.

They stood looking at a half a dozen or so cats. From tabbies to all shades of black, white and ginger. Some really fluffy and some sleek and shiny. It seemed to Colin they were all adult cats. He was about to ask Patsy their ages when a bolt of lightning hit him hard. Well actually, it was a cat. A solid fluffy grey creature clung on to his shoulder, staring at him.

Patsy quickly lifted the cat off Colin. "Oh, the blighter! He sprang from the climbing frame. Did he claw you? Any damage done?"

Colin noticed that Patsy was trying not to grin as he answered, "Nothing a couple of days in hospital won't fix."

They both went into peals of laughter. It occurred to Colin that he hadn't laughed like that for a very long time.

'I think perhaps the cat has chosen you, what do you reckon?"

Colin looked down at the bruiser of a cat that was now wrapping itself around his legs and making the friendliest of noises. He bent down and picked him up.

"Looks like you're right. Look at the size of him. He's a right bruiser. Hey, that's a good name for him. 'Bruiser'. What do you think of that, cat? How old is he anyway, do you know?"

Patsy realised she was staring at Colin. The unexpected mix of his very strong masculinity and gentleness had come as a shock, and she shook her head to clear the unexpected feelings.

"The old couple who brought him in said he was about three. He has been neutered of course. They were moving to live with family in Australia. The cat wasn't welcome there. Sad really, but their loss your gain. I think Bruiser is a perfect name, and if you ever shorten it to 'Bru' the neighbours will just think you need a beer."

"Very funny. Right, Bruiser it is." Colin grinned back at her. "Now Patsy, can I collect him after Boxing Day? I've promised family to spend Christmas with them. Is that okay with you?

As they went back to the house to discuss costs and get contact numbers he said, "By the way, I'm quite handy with a hammer and maybe I could give you a hand to fix up the cattery. That is, if it suits you?"

Patsy's eyes sparkled. "It sure would. Looks like you'll gain a cat, but I might have myself a new friend and a handyman to boot. This looks like being a really good Christmas after all!"

"I think it'll be a really great Christmas," Colin agreed. "I reckon it's a win-win situation for both of us, and Bruiser! Do you think we could seal the deal with another glass of your ginger beer?"

Patsy nodded her agreement, and happily led the way back to the house to do just that.

YOU CAN'T ALWAYS CHOOSE.

The heat from the golden globular sun was intense. For a split second the woman glanced up towards the heat source, trapped within its glare like a beetle about to be squashed beneath a heavy boot.

She took from her shirt pocket a grubby scrap of cloth, perhaps once a man's handkerchief, then slammed her spade into the unyielding soil. Lifting up her frayed sun-hat she wiped away the sweat that trickled from her forehead, seeking her eyes as if to blind her. There, that was a little better. A small moan of pain escaped her dry lips, as hands on her lower back, she slowly straightened, arching her back for relief.

"Mad dogs and Englishmen," she quoted, then laughing heartily added, "And mad women too." With a satisfied glance at the work begun, she picked up her spade and went towards the inviting dark of the bush. On reaching the shade she picked up a backpack and took out a water bottle, gratefully gulping down the cool liquid.

An observer would have had a hard time describing the woman. In her mid-to-late forties she certainly didn't make any attempt to look attractive. At first glance she appeared plain, with hair a frizzled mix of sun-faded blonde and freckles adorning all the skin that could be seen. Beneath a rather patrician nose a generous mouth softened her face and fine smile lines proved she had once smiled often. It was her eyes that lifted her from plain to rather unusual. They glittered with flecks of gold within their oval shape. A touch of the orient perhaps? Her figure was strong as mother earth, big-breasted, tall and solid.

The area she worked had been naturally bare, or perhaps once many years ago someone had cleared away trees. Maybe for a whare, a pioneer's hut, who knows? To Libby it seemed the perfect place for a vegetable garden, sheltered from the shattering southerly wind that at times roared in from the sea. She lifted the pack onto her back and her boots crunched the undergrowth as she wound her way through ancient trees that reached forever upwards.

She didn't have far to walk home. Ramshackle it may be, but still it was hers. A welcome mewing greeted her as a sleek black cat crawled out from under the porch of the house. She patted the fawning creature as it wrapped itself around her legs. "You're not silly, are you Missy? You know to stay out of the sun. Not like your Mum, eh?" With relief she sat on the rickety steps to pull off her boots and sweaty socks. "Come on then, let's get cleaned up."

Inside the small cabin she removed her shirt and half-filled the kitchen sink with cold water. No luxuries like a bathroom here, let alone hot water from a tap. Washing herself with a flannel she left her skin to dry, enjoying the brief respite from the heat. She never wore a bra, enjoying the feel of freedom this gave her. Living on the Barrier there was no need for such regimentation and folks here certainly didn't worry about such things. Anyway, she didn't get to mix much with people, preferring her own company, and Missy's of course.

Growing up, Libby had learned a little of the early family connection to the Great Barrier, way back in her great-grandparents' day.

An island in the outer Hauraki Gulf, just a hundred kilometres north-east of Auckland, life had been harsh in the 1920's –a bit different now. Libby had visited the island a couple of times. She had been impressed with the laid-back lifestyle and the few people she'd met. Now she was glad she had come here. For once she had made the right choice.

Later, a clean T-shirt on, she sat eating lunch considering what she should do next. Not that she always did what she should, in fact thinking about it; she seldom did. The old sofa beckoned her to come and rest. The minute she flopped into its cushioning valley, Missy leapt on top of her. "Okay girl, just for a few minutes." Pushing the cat down to one side, Libby closed her eyes.

It was the fly that woke her, dratted persistent thing. Moving Missy she went for the fly-swat. Whack–that settled that.

The folder sat on the table as always, taunting her. Pick me up, get on with it, what's wrong with you? Her conscience was never far away.

Sometimes Libby wondered if she was losing her marbles, talking to the cat and to herself. Or was it just the loneliness? Over a year ago she had bitten the bullet and made the major decision to do what *she* wanted for once. She'd had enough of a life of being controlled by others' wants and needs, though some of this she acknowledged had been her own bloody fault. Too many bad choices.

She listened to the birds and Missy's low contented purr, then shook her head to clear away negative thoughts, sat at the table and opened the folder. She looked down at what she had started – her memories poured onto paper. She needed Davy to understand. She picked up her pen.

Libby at just eighteen knew she had to get away from home. An unwanted, late-in-life child, her mother often shouted at her. 'You should never have been born.' Even all these years later, she remembered the hurt.

She had been about twelve, when sharing a changing room at a beach with her mum, she had turned to grab her towel. Not meaning to, she had seen her mother front on, totally nude. Libby had gasped with horror at the twisted centre that should have been her mother's stomach, the knotted scar pale pink against her white skin.

"What are you staring at?" her mother had shouted. "This is what you caused, making sure I didn't have any more brats like you," and she spun Libby around so hard she had hit the concrete wall. You don't forget a thing like that.

Libby couldn't wait to grow up and leave the house. Marriage seemed the answer; a bad mistake. Her first and only boyfriend Alan was just nineteen, not even out of his plumbing apprenticeship. All marriage meant to him was having sexual gratification on tap. Awfully disappointing too, if you asked Libby. Nothing like the Mills & Boon books she read. Neither she nor Alan had considered fully the responsibilities of marriage, let alone the chance of becoming parents. The inevitable happened when less than a year later, their child was born.

After a long, traumatic struggle, Libby finally pushed out a nine-pound son. His cries loudly pronounced anger at being thrust into this brightly lit world. Libby was totally drained, but on holding her baby felt a surge of utter triumph. Her spirits lifted as she told him he would always be wanted, always loved. The child was christened David.

Davy was only two years old when his father scarpered, never to be seen again. There was a rumour that he'd gone to Australia. Libby had no time to sit and weep, she'd needed to make decisions and quickly. She was lucky; a friend mentioned a farming family that needed a woman to housekeep and cook the evening meal, and a cottage was part of the deal. Libby applied for and got the job.

Davy was a placid, happy child and the family treated them well. Over the next three years Libby bought a cheap car and gradually built up a small nest egg, but she was restless. With Davy nearing school age Libby decided the time was right to move on.

For five years Libby and Davy moved on from one small town to another. She always managed to find a job and somewhere for them to bunk down. A rough life, though Davy seemed quite content. Libby didn't remain celibate for long. She craved affection but this time she took care to ensure the 'pill' was never forgotten. No more babies for her! Still, something remained missing. She never had a sexually satisfying relationship though she got pretty good at pretending. What, she often wondered, was wrong with her?

A move to the small, rather quaint gold mining town of Waihi led to a job in a rest home. Libby had worked as a carer before, and had good references. The work was physically hard and mentally demanding at times but she loved the old folk, some of whom never got a visitor; poor things. Libby enjoyed bringing them a brighter life and a lot of laughter.

108

Davy settled into school well and they loved the wee miner's cottage they rented. Together they grew a flourishing vegie garden and eventually Libby felt this could be the place they'd settle in for good. Proof of this was when Libby finally gave in to the boy's request for a dog. And so Sam, a dog of very mixed lineage, joined the family. He became Davy's dog, most definitely, even sleeping at night on a rug beside his bed. Life at long last was coming right.

Then came the year that Davy turned twelve and started college. Since moving to Waihi, Libby had been out on the odd date, but nothing meaningful. She was loth to complicate the serene life she and Davy enjoyed. The years flew by, peaceful, just what Libby wanted. She'd asked Davy several times what he wanted to do after leaving college. Varsity or what? Davy had shrugged. "I don't know. I haven't made my mind up yet."

At work one morning Libby was introduced to a new staff member, Annie. She was of average height with the trim boyish body of a model. In contrast to her lightly tanned skin, a mass of unruly auburn hair tumbled to her shoulders. When Annie looked at her with eyes of the deepest blue, Libby felt the strangest feeling–almost *déjà vu*. Annie smiled and an instant connection was made.

Annie was twelve years older than Libby and had lived all her life in Waihi. She had never married and after her father died suddenly, remained living at home to keep her mother company. When her mum was diagnosed with Parkinson's, Annie vowed to look after her and never to send her into care; and this she had done. Now Annie was alone except for her cat, hence this job.

The two women were to become very good friends, enjoying picnics at the beach and bush walks, and the occasional meal out, always with Davy in tow. He enjoyed Annie's company and the attention she gave him. She became like an aunt to him and in return he taught her many useful hints for using her computer.

The year Davy turned seventeen he made a decision. He was going to apply for a place as an Officer Cadet in the NZ Army. His school grades were very good, he said confidently. He was physically fit, school rugby saw to that, and he wanted to travel the world. Strange as it might seem he liked discipline, preferring to know where he stood in the scheme of things. When he told Libby she was surprised but rather proud of his positive approach to life.

Davy's application went in and the wait began. Would he get an interview, and then, would he be accepted as a trainee cadet?

A few weeks later Davy went on a weekend school trip to the big smoke –Auckland. He was looking forward to visiting the Auckland Museum, Kelly Tarlton's Aquarium and Rangitoto Island – choice, he reckoned.

Annie decided to cook dinner for Libby one evening and Libby looked forward to good conversation as well as the meal. Annie was a fantastic cook. Lots of CD's too with their shared love of classical music.

Dinner and wine were perfect, and having discussed work, music and movies, the talk turned to Davy and his future. Annie too was very proud of him. Dinner over, Libby settled on the sofa. She thought, this is what I love about Annie, everything we do together is enjoyable. Wow! Was that a revelation?

Annie was bringing the wine over to top up their glasses and she stood still, looking down lovingly at Libby. They both knew. No words were needed.

The next morning they discussed the situation honestly, their main concern being Davy. They didn't want to hurt him. Just leaving home and going into the Army would be hard enough, without having to cope with a mother who was, well, different. It was agreed that for at least a year they would carry on as they always had, each living in their own home with nothing changed. Continuing to appear as just good friends. Maybe one day Davy would even sense the situation and be okay with it. They could only hope.

How naïve they were.

Over dinner one night Davy told Libby about a new boy at school. He pulled a face as he said, "He's queer. You know Mum, a bloody poof. My mate Johnno called him a name and had to go to the Head for it.

"That dirty bastard gets away with his creepy ways and Johnno, who's a real good bloke, gets done. Not fair I reckon. That sort of weirdo make me want to throw up. They should be put away somewhere, where they can't try their dirty tricks on people, don't you reckon?"

Libby muttered something probably unintelligible and changed the subject.

In bed that night she tossed and turned. If Davy felt that strongly about someone he barely knew, what the hang would he think of her? She had to talk to Annie.

She and Annie shared the same work shift the next day, and after they finished Libby suggested a drink at the pub, somewhere neutral seeming a good idea. They went round and around in circles trying to sort out what they should do. They both agreed that for now Davy must come first; he was after all, still very young. Nothing was solved. Both women were miserable but decided it would be best to see less of each other for now. There would still be the occasional 'family' outings to enjoy, with no problems arising. This then was the way to go in the meantime.

Davy's Army interview in Auckland went well and some weeks later his letter of acceptance arrived. Eleven months in camp confirmed – Davy was over the moon. He had a list of what to take and Libby thought it hilarious that this included, amongst other things, an iron! Finally the day came when, all packed up, Libby and Annie saw him off at the bus-stop. They tried not to cry for his sake, but noticed even Davy rubbing his eyes as he clambered on the bus. He would write and so would they.

Davy didn't get much time for writing letters and those he did write were brief. The meals were great, the guys he shared with okay and he was getting super fit.

He had been at Waiouru Military Camp for a few months when his intake was given a three-day pass. He shared the army barrack with several other guys, one who came from Pauanui, north of Waihi. Paul had a car and offered to drop Davy off on his way home.

They checked out later than expected, eventually getting away in the afternoon, so by the time they arrived in Waihi it was after ten o'clock. When they pulled up at Davy's, the house was in darkness. Not a problem, as Davy had his own key. Thanking Paul for the ride, Davy went down the back path. He noticed Annie's car was there. She often stayed over after a wine or two. Better than getting ticketed by a cop for being over the limit, she always said. Unlocking the door, he let himself in. The house was in darkness except for a faint light coming from his mother's room. She was probably reading.

Davy put down his pack and with a grin quietly walked down the hall. Wait till Mum saw him, boy what a surprise she'd have.

Davy stood in the doorway hardly grasping what he saw. His mother and Annie, bare bodies moving sinuously, so engrossed in each other they hadn't even noticed him. A moan escaped his lips, becoming the wail of a hurt animal. He stumbled away from the sight as the women both called – "Davy!"

As he grabbed his pack they came after him, pulling on dressing gowns, babbling, making no sense. He couldn't look at them, felt utter repulsion for what he had seen, for what they were.

"You make me sick," he shouted and looking at Libby added, "You're no mother of mine, I never want to see you again, ever!" and he stormed out of the house slamming the door behind him.

All Libby could think about now was Davy; he had to come first. Annie left for home and Libby got in the car to look for him. She drove through the streets, even driving some way south in case he was walking back to camp. As she drove Libby chastised herself for what she had done. Poor Davy. Finally Libby gave up, guessing Davy must have hitched a ride back to camp. He had gone. She wept all the way home. For her son, the hurt she had caused him, as well as for Annie and herself.

The letters Libby wrote to Davy were never answered. In desperation she contacted the Army Base Commander. Of course she just said she and her son had a falling out, and she only wanted to make sure he was all right. The Commander assured her that Cadet Baxter was fine, he was doing well. He said parents would be invited to the graduation ceremony and with that, she had to be satisfied.

Knowing it was for the best, Annie resigned from her work at the rest home. Both women missed each other terribly. Eventually, very slowly, the hurt eased. Occasionally they would see each other; when out shopping, in the library or in the street. It was a jolt each time. They spoke briefly, always avoiding full eye contact.

Libby received a letter confirming her son had passed his Cadetship, and inviting her to attend the graduation ceremony. A few days later she got a letter from Davy. He was aware of the invitation she would have received, and asked her not to attend as she was not welcome. It was simply signed, David.

Libby did not attend.

She continued to write to Davy though she never got replies until finally she too stopped writing.

At work one day another carer said, "I was sorry to hear about Annie. Lovely lady I always thought. Good friend of yours isn't she Libby?"

"Yes she is, but why, what's wrong with Annie? I haven't seen her for a while."

"I heard its heart problems, bad by the sound of it."

Libby struggled to concentrate on her work, thinking about Annie sick and all alone. The day couldn't go quickly enough. Straight after work she went to Annie's place, let herself in and found Annie in the sunroom, lying back in her chair, seemingly dozing. Libby noted the shallow breathing and pinched lips, the pale face and her hands, so bony now. Libby looked at the walker and the side table with tablets and water. She stood there with tears streaming down her face for her dear, dear Annie.

Annie stirred and opened her eyes. "Libby, my love, please don't cry."

They talked for a long time. Eventually, Libby got Annie to agree to come home with her. After phoning Annie's doctor and getting his full approval, she brought Annie back to her house and set her up in the sunniest bedroom. She drove back and forth from Annie's bringing all the belongings Annie needed and set up a lazy-boy chair by the window in the lounge, where she could sit and watch the birds on the back lawn. Sam, in his old-age, making half-hearted attempts to chase them.

Libby became Annie's carer. At work she organised reduced hours, to give her more time with Annie. The District Nurse came regularly as did her doctor, but it was Libby who helped Annie with showering.

The months went by and the time came when Annie also needed help with toileting. This Libby did with tender loving care.

Eventually Annie could not be left alone and Libby resigned from her job. There was no way she would let anyone else look after her precious Annie.

As she weakened, Annie talked to Libby about the past. About Davy and how she would give anything to see him again. To tell him how sorry she felt being the cause of his, and Libby's parting. She asked Libby to write to him one more time–for her sake. Libby did but received no reply.

As the sun rose one morning Annie passed away in Libby's arms. A peaceful passing, the end of a very special friendship. Her last words to Libby were, 'Always loved you.' Old Sam was sitting by her side as usual, comforting her. It was strange that within a few days Libby found Sam on the rug by Davy's bed, passed away in the night. She shed more tears. Her last link to Davy was gone.

Libby returned to work, immersing herself in her job as if keeping busy would ease the pain and heal all wounds. Several months later she was to find that in her will, Annie had left her home and all her possessions to her. Now Libby could make a change, go away, and live somewhere else; but where? And then she recalled the Great Barrier. She drove to Auckland and took the boat trip across, looking for a small place, a bit of land. Perhaps here she would find peace.

Libby put down the pen and rubbed her tired eyes. Well, it was done. Whether or not Davy ever read this, and most importantly, came to understand what had been, was another question. Would he realise that one does not always get to choose who to love?

Libby stood up and glanced at the wall clock. "Tide should be full in now. A swim, that's what I need," she said to Missy. She changed into togs and tossing a towel around her shoulders, slid her feet into sandals. Walking down the rutted driveway she paused to study the name carved into a large chunk of driftwood. She had carved this herself and proudly hung it on the cabbage tree.

As always, Libby smiled as she read the sign.

ANNIE'S.

She would certainly approve.

SING ME A SONG

When their fourth child was born – a girl at last to David and Maria Bonnington – Maria was determined to give the child a very special name, and so the baby was christened Geraldine Florence Anna Maria Bonnington. She would always be called Geraldine in full and she rather liked that. There were to be two more children after her, another brother then the last child, another girl.

The family may have had little money but their children were healthy and happy. The bungalow in Devonport, on Auckland's North Shore, was a house full of shared laughter and at times, tears. A humble home, but full of the warmth of love.

David Bonnington worked as a wharfie on the Auckland docks, crossing the Waitemata harbour on the ferries to get to work. He was a tall man, and muscular as the result of hard work, with a booming voice to match his size, the exact opposite to his wife Maria. Even after the birth of six children she remained a tiny scrap of a lady. Small she may have been, but Maria too was strong, not only in health but in spirit. She instilled in her children, her aspirations for them to do well in life.

Devonport was a beautiful place in which to live. There was not only Torpedo Bay for swimming, but also the Windsor Reserve – a popular place for picnics, and the Esplanade for a pleasant stroll. Wherever you went, you were never far from the bracing tang of the sea. The Devonport wharf was popular with children and adults alike, where they often caught some decent sized fish. The townsfolk were friendly and many forms of the arts flourished including writers, poets, musicians, artists, potters and sculptors. Although only a short ferry ride to the big city of Auckland, the suburb had the feel of a separate entity, a character endorsed and enjoyed by the residents. In 1959, the opening of the Auckland Harbour Bridge to Northcote had little impact on the residents of Devonport. Unless they were heading south, they still used the ferry boats to reach Auckland city.

Having the New Zealand Naval Base at Devonport also made the area special, with smartly-presented sailors causing a fluttering of many a young girl's heart. Sometimes this resulted in wedding bells and sometimes in heartache; such was life!

Geraldine Bonnington may have been very like her mother in many ways, but not in looks. She was taller – well everyone was taller than her mum – and had flaming red hair, the only redhead in the family; a throwback from an Irish great-great-grandmother, she was told. Geraldine would much rather have had nondescript brown hair any day. A modest girl, she didn't realise how striking she was with her hair, creamy skin and rich green eyes.

It was when Geraldine progressed from Primary School to Grammar that she took a serious interest in singing. Her mother's great love was playing the piano, and taught by her mother, Geraldine often accompanied her, their duets a delight to the rest of the family. As Geraldine matured so did her voice. She sang effortlessly, and as she grew older her voice gained the full purity of a strong soprano. No note too high to reach, with the 'clarity of a bellbird' her father once said, and he was right.

After her first year at Takapuna Grammar, she joined the school choir and often sang the solo part. Once singing, her normal shyness vanished, the music taking her to heights of contented bliss. The choir master saw her potential and asked if private singing lessons were possible. Geraldine told him definitely not! Knowing there was little money to spare she wouldn't even consider asking her father.

Geraldine left school at sixteen and her search for work began. She was most excited when her mother read out an advertisement for a shop assistant required at Lewis Eady's, the well-known music store in the centre of Auckland city. The very next day Geraldine went in person to apply for the position, and was over the moon when she was accepted. Her knowledge of music and her piano-playing capabilities, along with her well-groomed appearance and polite manner, had impressed her future employers. Geraldine was now a young working lady.

For two years she led a busy, contented life. There was not only her job, but she also helped her mother with the housework and cooking. There was swimming which she loved, and every day after work she exercised Jamie, the family's Cocker Spaniel. Movies at the Victoria Theatre Geraldine thought wonderful – preferably musicals of course! She and her best friend Daphne would walk home after these, dancing along the footpath and singing at the top of their voices, laughing at their attempts to emulate the movie stars they had seen on the screen.

Geraldine did, however, miss singing in a choir, so she began to make enquiries as to choirs in their area. The answer came from Daphne who excitedly told her about a newly-formed Devonport Community Choir seeking more members.

The girls went along to the next choir practise and were made most welcome. On that first night, Geraldine noticed very little of the other singers; she just enjoyed sharing the music and the performance of the very talented conductor. She, a Miss Taylor, bounced around enthusiastically waving her baton in the air with verve, making the session great fun.

Geraldine had been a member of the choir for a month or so when one day, a man came into Lewis Eady's asking for a particular piece of sheet music for piano, and she had a vague feeling that she'd seen him before.

He was what some people would term an albino. His hair so fair it was almost white, his eyebrows and eyelashes, she noticed, the same. His eyes were a clear pale blue and a scattering of freckles brushed his cheeks.

A tinge of red covered these as he spoke to Geraldine. "Aren't you one of the members of the Devonport Community Choir?"

Geraldine looked up at him. "Why yes, I am. I thought you looked familiar, are you a pianist?" Then she looked at the sheet music in her hand. "Of course you must be, or you wouldn't be buying this, would you? How silly of me."

He laughed in a kindly manner. "By the way, I'm Patrick Carron, and you are?"

"Geraldine," she said. "Geraldine Bonnington."

"I'm very pleased to meet you. Yes, I do play piano, just for my own enjoyment you know, though my parents also seem to enjoy my playing. What about you?"

They chatted briefly as his purchase was made. "See you at the next choir practice?" he asked, and Geraldine smiled.

"Yes, of course." Saying goodbye, she went on to serve another customer.

Arriving home from work she told her mother, "At work today I met a chap who sings in the same choir as me. Patrick Carron is his name and he lives in Devonport too."

"I've heard of the Carron family," her mother said. "Live up on the hill. The father works in the office at the local council. They only had the one child, a son, that's probably him. I think they sent him to Varsity, so they must be quite well off." She stopped peeling vegetables for a moment. "Made an impression on you did he Geraldine?" she asked with raised eyebrows.

Ignoring her mother's questioning look Geraldine shrugged. "Not especially, but I suppose I'll see him at Wednesday's practise. Well, I'd better get changed now Mum and take Jamie for his walk." She bent down to pat the dog who waited patiently.

This was the beginning of a close friendship that gradually grew deeper. Both sets of parents were pleased to see their son and daughter 'going steady'. Patrick was six years older than Geraldine. 'A sensible age difference,' her father commented.

Music was the couple's common bond, and as the Community choir became established, they were in high demand to perform for organisations, hospitals and rest-homes. Geraldine and Patrick very much enjoyed the satisfaction this brought. At times they would sing a duet; his rich deep baritone the perfect foil for her sweet voice.

Out of the blue one day, Patrick called Geraldine, 'Birdie'.

She laughed. "What did you call me?" she asked, having heard full well what he'd said.

"You sing beautifully my love, like I imagine a lark would. Clear and pure, my dear, dear Birdie." He kissed her cheek. "You don't mind do you?"

Geraldine smiled. "This is the first time in my life I've been called anything other than Geraldine, and I think it's rather lovely. Of course I don't mind, I don't mind at all."

Geraldine found herself wondering why somehow she felt let down by Patrick. Actually, she really did know. It was Patrick's kiss on the cheek. His reticence, his – dare she admit it even to herself – his seeming lack of passion. Heck, what was wrong with her? He was a very decent man and she was, as her parents had said, fortunate to have such a well-mannered, considerate boyfriend.

Patrick worked as a lawyer, for a large firm of Barristers and Solicitors, and he was very ambitious. He intended to one day become a partner in the firm and Geraldine felt sure he would achieve his aim.

One evening as they walked arm in arm along the Esplanade, Patrick told Geraldine some special news. He'd been asked by one of the partners to take on a more senior role. The company had a new client in shipping, and this required one-on-one attention. If Patrick agreed to this, it would of course include a higher salary to reflect his added responsibilities. Sensibly, Geraldine thought, he had asked for time to consider this, although he already knew what his answer would be. Patrick knew not to appear too impetuous. "What do you think Birdie?" he asked.

"I think that's fantastic news Patrick, and of course you should take the offer, if it's what you want."

Patrick stopped walking and looked seriously at Geraldine. "There is one other thing, Birdie. With the extra money coming in, I think this is the right time to ask you. Would you do me the honour of becoming my wife?" He smiled down at her. "I do care for you Birdie, and feel sure we are well matched. If you agree you would make me a very happy man, and I'm sure my parents would be delighted."

Geraldine stood speechless for a moment, her head spinning with thoughts. Of course she should accept; she cared for him too. Smiling up at Patrick she said, "Yes my love, I will marry you." She tilted up her face for a kiss, ready to fling her arms around Patrick's neck. He reached down and holding her shoulders, lightly brushed her lips with his. "Marvellous, Birdie, can't wait to tell the parents. Come on, let's do that now." And swinging her hand in his they turned back for home.

The engagement ring was chosen and the announcement put in the local paper as well as in the NZ Herald. Patrick always did everything in the proper manner. He suggested an engagement period of twelve months as there was so much to organise. A home to be found, then wedding arrangements and so on. He would see to all of that, Birdie needn't worry about anything.

At their next practice the fellow choir members congratulated the happy couple. The choir had just received their new uniforms and they did look smart. The women were in full-length pure white robes with a crossed sash of deep blue. The men wore dress shirts in the same silky blue colour as the sashes, along with light grey trousers and ties. The first time Patrick saw Geraldine in her robe he could hardly take his eyes off her. "My beautiful Birdie," he said. "Perfect, my very own Birdie."

Why this bothered Geraldine she wasn't sure, but somehow it made her feel like a… a possession. Oh dear, what was wrong with her?

During the next twelve months Patrick put down a deposit on a small cottage, and now had a mortgage to pay. The house was just down the hill from his parents' home. Good to be near Mother and Father, Patrick had said.

The wedding plans were a cause of some concern to Patrick's mother. She knew of the financial restraints of Geraldine's parents, and requested a meeting with them. After a lengthy discussion, it was agreed that Patrick's folks be allowed to contribute to the wedding costs. After all, as his mother pointed out, Patrick had to consider his position in the firm. Appearances were most important, and a small wedding with basic catering simply would not do. And so all was arranged.

The wedding day was to be in October on Labour Weekend. Everyone prayed for fine weather, and they were greatly relieved when the day dawned clear with just the gentlest of breezes. It was a nervous bride who walked up the aisle towards her husband-to-be, a cascading bouquet trembling in her hands.

Geraldine vaguely noticed the church was full, as the organist brought the wedding march to a final crescendo. Then the elderly minister asked the oft-repeated words, "Who is it that giveth this woman to be married?" Her father gave his clear answer and passed her to Patrick.

Geraldine watched her new husband as he signed the wedding register, and all she could think was, when the minister said, 'You can now kiss the bride,' why hadn't Patrick kissed her like a husband should, strongly, firmly? Then she chastised herself for being so critical. That was just not Patrick's way.

After the wedding breakfast, they left for their new home where they changed into going-away clothes. With the car packed, they were soon on their way to Te Puru on the Coromandel Peninsula, where Patrick had rented a bach for their honeymoon.

Geraldine was not ignorant of the facts of life. No-one was these days, with movies and television and rather explicit books. Still, she was nervous, very nervous. She reassured herself that Patrick would be gentle and considerate. After all, he was such a gentleman.

The drive was pleasant and Geraldine began to relax. Arriving at the cottage, they settled in and Patrick said, "I thought we would eat at the little restaurant by the beach tonight."

The evening was most enjoyable; perhaps the wine helped. Geraldine seldom drank alcohol, but this was a very special occasion and she began to unwind. The meal over, they slowly meandered back to the cottage. Patrick showered first and came out to the lounge wearing silk paisley pyjamas.

"Your turn Birdie," he said and went into the bedroom.

Geraldine knew she had to get out of the shower soon, as the water was beginning to cool. She quickly dried herself and put on the white satin nightgown she had chosen for this, their first night together. She trembled, and it wasn't just from the cold.

The loss of her virginity proved she'd been right to be scared, though she never for a minute had expected Patrick to be like this. For this was not the Patrick she knew. This was a sadistic, cruel monster who raped her repeatedly. Bit her and twisted her flesh, ignoring her pleas for him to stop.

Blood stained the beautiful nightgown, matching the bleeding of her heart.

After what seemed an eternity, he rolled away from her and fell asleep, leaving her to weep.

'What have I done, what have I done?' she asked herself.

As the dawn began to lighten the room, Geraldine finally slept.

She was woken by the sound of Patrick whistling. She hastily got up and covered herself with her dressing gown. She showered and dressed, bundling the stained nightdress away out of sight.

She was amazed to hear Patrick's voice calling, "Is that you up and about Birdie?" as if the night before had never happened. He kissed her on the cheek saying, "Now, what shall we do today, Birdie?"

This was to become Patrick's regular behaviour. His personality changed at night to brutal domination, as if he was another person. Geraldine wanted the 'honeymoon' to be over, wanted to go home. Perhaps, she thought, once he was back at work he would stop his perverted ways and treat her more kindly. She could only hope.

Within a few short weeks Geraldine knew she was pregnant. Instead of telling Patrick she kept the fact hidden for as long as possible, frightened of how he would react. But the time came when Geraldine knew she would have to resign from her job, and she had to tell him.

She was greatly relieved at his reaction. "I will be a father," Patrick said. "I'll have a son to teach and train to be a man, and Mother will be very pleased." Geraldine shuddered at his voice. Was this all a baby meant to him? Another person to control? God help them both, her and the child.

Friends and families knew nothing of Geraldine's trauma. She would have been too ashamed to speak of this to anyone, even her mother or her best friend Daphne.

Patrick was at work when Geraldine went into labour. After her waters had broken she phoned her doctor, and was told that when the pains were less than five minutes apart she should go to the hospital. She then rang Patrick at the office. "I'm on my way," he said.

Patrick arrived and just stared at her, really oddly. "This'll be my last chance for a while," he said, and grasping her he dragged her into the bedroom. Pushing her down onto the bed he brutally used her as a vessel for his satisfaction, then finished, pulled her to her feet. "Time to go," he said. As another spasm of pain gripped her, Geraldine moaned involuntarily, and seeing Patrick's twisted smile, she knew he was enjoying her suffering.

It was several hours later that the baby was born. Geraldine cried with relief when she heard the doctor saying, "You have a daughter, Mrs. Carron, a beautiful healthy little girl." Geraldine's first thought was, thank heavens – a girl. Not a boy for Patrick to mould to his sick ways.

Patrick was a most unhappy man. He scowled down at Geraldine as he stood at the end of her bed. "I shall tell my parents," he told her, and left without even looking at his new daughter.

Her time in hospital was utter bliss for Geraldine. Totally relaxed for the first time in ages, she enjoyed bonding with her infant.

Patrick had been so convinced the child would be a boy that names for a girl had never even been discussed. Geraldine knew what she wanted the baby to be called – Angela. A perfect name for her little angel, and Maria, after her mother.

The day Patrick brought her home from the hospital, Geraldine sat in a comfortable chair to breastfeed the baby. When Patrick entered the lounge and saw her he shouted, "Get out of here, I've never seen anything so revolting. You can use the sunroom for that purpose. Don't ever let me see you doing that again."

Geraldine was happy to oblige.

A few days later, Patrick informed her that he would be sleeping in the guest room from now on. It was a respite as far as Geraldine was concerned. There was a further change in Patrick – he no longer called her Birdie, but Geraldine. Some nights she heard him arrive home very late and never knew where he had been; and she didn't care. At least life was bearable now, and she had her beautiful wee daughter to love.

Angela was just six months old when Patrick informed Geraldine of changes to be made. He had been asked by the senior partners to establish a branch in Melbourne and he had agreed. He would buy an apartment there as he had no intention of returning to New Zealand. Geraldine and the child would of course, remain in New Zealand. He had arranged with his lawyer for her to have a regular, quite generous income, and in time he would organise divorce proceedings. This was to be done in an agreeable manner, of course. Geraldine could remain in the house until the child's education was finished, university included, and after that, the house would be sold and the proceeds divided equally between them. He asked only that Geraldine agree to tell their parents they had reached an amicable parting of the ways.

Geraldine remained quiet for a few moments, staring hard at Patrick. Why hadn't she noticed before? His eyes; they were empty cold spaces, devoid of emotion. She almost felt sorry for him – he would never know love. She hoped her face did not reveal her relief.

"I'm in agreement with all you say; and of course I trust you to handle this in the proper manner, Patrick," she said. "After all, haven't you always acted with the utmost decorum?"

The reddening of his face showed that the barb had hit home, and this was confirmed by the slamming of the door as he left the house.

The sudden loud noise woke Angela and she whimpered. Geraldine hurried to pick her up and smiled down at her, kissing her lovingly. "Just you and me now my sweet, just you and me," she told her, and with a lighter heart she began to sing a soothing lullaby.

LOVE & UNDERSTANDING

The wind blew her hair back from her forehead and she whooped with delight. As she concentrated on keeping her scooter steady, her mother's string bag with the few groceries in it swung from side to side.

The road down from the grocer's was steep, a challenge the small girl enjoyed. The corner came up even quicker than expected and she steered around it in a wide arc; far too wide! Mrs. Baxter, the next-door neighbour, appeared right in front of her.

Mrs. Baxter squealed and shouted as the scooter missed her by a whisker. "You stupid girl! You're an absolute menace. Wait till I talk to your mother."

"Sorry, sorry," the child called over her shoulder as she scooted on home. Shivers, she thought to herself. Now I'm in for it, in trouble again.

Home. She stopped and leant the scooter against the high hedge as she unlatched the heavy wooden gate. Then after pushing the scooter through and closing the gate behind her, she scooted down the side path and around to the back door.

She grabbed the string kit and raced inside.

"Mum, Mum, I've got the shopping."

Her mother answered from the kitchen. "Alright Milly. I heard you the first time. Always in a rush aren't you?"

Milly put the shopping down on the kitchen table and flopped onto a seat. She was a skinny child, almost waifish. Dark hair cut short contrasted with fair skin. Plain, one would think, until she looked at you with those big hazel eyes, then she became interesting.

Her mum took the half pound of butter, half loaf of bread and the jar of Marmite out of the bag.

"Oh Milly, look at this. How did the bread get so squashed?" she asked.

Milly hesitated before answering. Should she confess now about nearly running down Mrs. Baxter or say nothing and hope Mrs. Baxter never told her mum? Deciding on the latter she said, "It's pretty hard to keep the scooter steady with the bag swinging about, Mum."

The mother studied her child. The unexpected and certainly unintended baby had arrived just after her fortieth birthday. She had thought her child-bearing days were over. Now here she was fifty years old and having to cope with a whirlwind of a girl – a real tomboy. She sighed. "Well, go and find something to do and let me get on with making this soup."

Milly wandered outside and plonked herself down on the back steps. What to do now, she asked herself. Then she remembered – the hut. There was work to be done, and she raced off to her dad's shed for some tools.

The family home was on the usual suburban Kiwi quarter-acre. Down behind the chook run, Milly cleared out a place under the trees and here she'd begun to make a hut.

Dad had given her some old bits of left-over timber, Pinex board, and the old wooden railing he'd removed from the front veranda. Today she would try and fit the piece of rusty roof iron over the top. Milly thought of having a snug hut to sit in and read, reading being her most favourite thing to do, next to riding her scooter. With a few nails and Dad's hammer the banging began.

From the kitchen her mum listened and guessed it would be Milly working on her hut. Oh well, at least it was keeping her out of mischief for a while. Then she heard the shrill sound of the front doorbell.

Opening the door she was surprised to see Mrs. Baxter standing there, hands on her very ample hips. "Good afternoon Mrs. Baxter," she greeted her. "And how are you these days? Do you want to come in?"

"No thank you Mrs. Parkins," came the reply. "This is not a social call. I've just come to see you about your daughter Milly. I was on my way to the grocers to do a bit of shopping, when she sped round the corner on her scooter and almost knocked me over. Really shook me up it did. She's a right menace that girl, and you should take the scooter off her; teach her a lesson. Either that or see that your hubby gives her a good tanning."

"I'm very sorry to hear you got such a fright Mrs. Baxter, and I will certainly talk to Milly, you can rest assured. I shall also talk to her father and I do apologise for your upset. Now if you'll excuse me, I have a pot of soup on the simmer. I should go and check it."

Saying goodbye to her neighbour Miriam Parkins closed the door. She turned the heat off under the soup and went looking for her horror of a child.

It was a terrified girl, who having been chastised for not confessing to her wrong-doings, now waited obediently in the bathroom. Milly knew from experience what was coming. From the window, she watched her mother stride down the back garden and break off a branch of the Monkey Apple hedge. She swished it experimentally in the air. Obviously not supple enough as she threw it away. The second piece it seemed would do. Milly felt sick with fear as her mother came back into the bathroom.

"Now Milly Parkins, bend over the bath."

The whipping began. With the first sting across her bloomered buttocks Milly flinched and straightened up. This only caused the whipping to continue around her upper legs as well as her bottom. She yelped, crying out. "Stop Mum, please stop." Finally, her mother's anger spent, the whipping was over.

Worse was to come. When her father was told of her behaviour he forbade her the use of her scooter for two whole weeks! Her freedom and fun curtailed.

That whipping Milly remembered well. It was to be only one of many, for somehow she continued getting into scrapes. She never meant to, it just happened. Lost school books, muddied shoes, bed not made, homework not done, ripped clothes from climbing trees. The list was long. And then about several months later, that fateful day arrived.

Milly didn't much like her Primary school. The main building where her class was appeared dark and forbidding. It was built from grey granite blocks, the small windows far too high up for small children to see out. The classroom got no sun and in winter the central potbelly coal burner did little to warm up the room.

Her teacher, a Mr. Dibble whose name caused much laughter and the making up of silly chants, was as forbidding as the room. Milly had never seen him smile and he was always quick to use his cane and the strap.

At school, Milly had formed a special friendship with Brenda. They had become good friends one day when Milly had gone across to the drinking fountain for a drink of water. There was a group of boys poking, laughing and mocking a girl much smaller than themselves. They were calling her stutter kid, over and over. Milly got mad and without stopping to think, pushed in between the boys and yanked the girl away from them. "Leave her alone," she'd shouted.

Milly had felt a fist strike her cheek, but just then a teacher had appeared and the bullies scattered. The girl Milly had rescued was Brenda, and from that day on their friendship was sealed.

Brenda was different to other kids. She could draw pictures that were really real-looking. Anything from animals to boats and beaches. Milly thought that wonderful. Brenda also had a slight stutter and didn't talk a lot, but with Milly she hardly stuttered at all.

When Milly found out that Brenda had no father, as he had died a couple of years ago, she became even more protective of her new friend.

There was only one problem, as the children saw it. Brenda lived a few miles away so used the school bus to get to school and back. Milly walked to school, so they couldn't play after school, and they so wished they could. Then one day Brenda had a brilliant idea. Why hadn't she thought of it before!

She had a bus ticket. She could click Milly on too. Brenda lived at Island Bay, right by the beach. They would have a great time. Her mum could take Milly home when she got home from work; it was as simple as that.

The girls were that excited, waiting for the end-of-day school bell to ring.

Once off the bus the girls walked down the steep hill to Brenda's house. She took a key from under a pot plant and opened the back door. Brenda told Milly that her brother would be home from college soon. They were used to looking after themselves until their mum got home from work.

Brenda changed into togs and gave Milly an old pair of hers to wear. Down at the beach they raced each other into the water, acting like playful porpoises, each showing off their swimming skills. They ducked each other under the water then ran along the beach kicking up the warm sand. In no time the sun dried them as they went walking over the rocks, checking rock pools and trying, unsuccessfully, to pull limpets off the sea-scored surface. They clambered up the zigzag path of the cliff-face and on reaching the top, sat looking across the water to the big city of Auckland. Brenda pointed out lots of places Milly had never heard of before. Milly couldn't help but notice Brenda hadn't stuttered once.

Hunger eventually drove them back to Brenda's house. Dressed again, they helped themselves to Weetbix soaked in heaps of milk, then went into Brenda's room where she showed Milly her album of drawings.

"You're going to be a famous artist one day Brenda, just you wait and see," Milly said. Brenda was chuffed but modest. The girls sat back on the bed and talked. They heard the door shutting as John, Brenda's big brother, arrived home. He poked his head around the door and Brenda explained who Milly was. Saying a brief hello, he left them alone.

Neither of the girls had a watch and it wasn't until Milly said to Brenda, "Ooh look, it's getting dark. What do you reckon the time is?" that they ran to the kitchen to check the big wall clock. It was almost six o'clock! Ye gods! Milly realised she was in big, big trouble.

Brenda said, "I thought Mum would have been home way before this, she must be working late. I'm so sorry Milly, it's all my fault you're stuck here."

With those words Milly burst into tears. "What can I do?" she asked.

"Come on Milly, let's go and talk to John."

Brenda's brother was no help at all. Of course they didn't have a phone. Very few people had phones in their houses. And even if they had, Milly's folks didn't anyway. There was nothing to do but wait, and hope Brenda's mum would soon be home.

The fun, like the sun, had gone from the day. Milly realised the enormity of what she had done.

She imagined her mum waiting and wondering where she was, her dad arriving home from work, and then what? Now Milly was really frightened. She realised she never should have come home with Brenda.

The banging on the front door made them all jump.

"That can't be Mum," said John. "She has a key. I'll see who it is. You girls stay here."

What a shock. John opened the door to see a helmeted policeman standing there and in a booming voice he asked if he could come in.

When the policeman; helmet tucked under his arm, followed John into the room Milly recognised him straight away. It was Constable Watson, the local bobby who lived not far from her home. There was even a cell built on the back of his property – often referred to by Milly's parents as an example of where 'bad' people were put. Milly's eyes were like saucers and she shook with fear.

"Hello young Milly Parkins," Constable Watson said, staring at her. "You, my girl, are in big trouble. What do you have to say for yourself?" The usually talkative Milly was, for once, speechless.

The two girls sobbed and clung to each other before Milly was bundled into the police car. Constable Watson lectured Milly all the way home. The worry and trouble she had caused her parents. The tracking down he had to do, to find out where she had gone. Her totally irresponsible manner in giving no thought to her parents, and on and on!

Milly thought the ride would never end. One part of her wanted to be home and yet she was sure she was in for the biggest hiding of her life. Eventually the ride was over. Milly was home.

His face like thunder, her father sent Milly into the sitting room and closed the door. Milly could vaguely hear Constable Watson talking to her parents and their murmured answers. Then the front door was shut and her father entered the sitting room. The lecture he gave her was almost word for word what the constable had said. By the time her father had finished, tears were rolling down Milly's face.

"I'm really sorry Dad. I just never thought what might happen. I promise I won't ever again go anywhere after school without asking you or Mum first."

"That's as may be girl," her father answered. "But you know you have to be punished. It's my duty as your father to make sure you never forget this day, and that you never worry your mother and me like this again."

He closed the door and took the wide leather belt from his trousers. He looped part of it around his broad hand. "Bend over the chair girl."

The belting began, interspersed with her father's comments. "You will never ever go anywhere after school without first asking us." Whack. "Do you understand?" Whack. "Do you promise to behave from now on?" Whack. Milly's cries drowned a lot of his words.

Down the hall in the kitchen, Milly's mother stood arms crossed, trembling. She got angry often with this troublesome child and chastised her as needed, but hearing her cries she hoped the belting would soon be over.

Twenty-four years later Milly stood in her own kitchen, shaking her head at her twelve-year-old son Max. He had arrived home covered in mud, wheeling – more like dragging – his bicycle. An explanation came hard and fast. No, he wasn't hurt. The front wheel was twisted from a collision with a corner of the Waimana Bridge, going downhill of course. Yes, probably going too fast! When he'd hit the corner of the bridge he'd gone up and over the railing, landing in the mangroves. Jolly lucky the tide was out at the time. Just think, he could've been drowned!

He stood there expecting his mum to give him a right dressing-down. Her decision to take the cost of repairs to his bike from his pocket money came as a relief. No TV and early to bed was harder, but he realised he was getting off pretty lightly. As Max went to get cleaned up he glanced back at his mum. She appeared to be deep in thought. Strange, she almost seemed to be grinning. He wondered what on earth she found amusing, given the telling off she'd just given him.

Milly saw her son staring at her and said sharply, "Go and get that muck off you Max, and make sure you leave the bathroom tidy." As he left the room she went back to remembering the scrapes she too had got into as a youngster. Probably one day she would tell Max just why he'd got off so lightly, the day he wrecked his bike. About her scooter incident, and why she and his 'Aunt' Brenda were such close friends.

I may be a mum, she thought; but I can still recall the fun times of my childhood, even if they did sometimes lead to hidings. I know children don't always stop to think – I didn't. Sometimes they have to learn the hard way – like I did. Nothing much changes from one generation to the next, she pondered. Except for punishment of course. Kids are lucky these days. Parents are not even allowed to give them a slap. A good thing? I wonder.

One thing I do know – kids are kids no matter what – that never changes. And parenting isn't just feeding and clothing. It's far more important to show love and understanding.

Milly sighed deeply. Wait till I tell Brenda about Max's latest scrape. She could just hear Brenda's laughter and her saying, 'I wonder who he could possibly take after?'

Milly sighed as the mothering instinct cut in. As far as she was concerned the crisis was over. Right now she had a hungry lad to look after.

"Max, when you're cleaned up, come and get your snack."

"Good one Mum, be there soon."

Milly put the jug on to make them both a cuppa. Well, that's sorted, all back to normal, at least for now. Tomorrow who knows, but, she shrugged her shoulders; tomorrow is another day.

ACHILLES HEEL

Big Billy Buxton lived alone with his mum Sal. It was said by the locals that as Billy grew he ate so much that there was never enough food for his dad to exist on and so the old man gradually faded away. It was true that Sal was a wisp of a woman, perhaps she also, had little enough food. A gusty breeze and she had to hang on to the nearest solid object to stop being blown away! To add substance to this theory Sal was often seen scrounging in the woods. Berries, mushrooms in season, watercress and puha all went in her basket, her jaws often munching as she harvested.

No wonder Billy was like the end of a barn; tall, rounded and solid. When he walked, his booted feet took strides twice the size of your average guy, and nobody ever disagreed with anything Billy said – even when he bragged about his conquests.

There wasn't a girl in town Billy hadn't had his way with, *he* reckoned, and not mentioning names, a few married women to boot. Here the menfolk in the pub would redden up and wriggle uncomfortably on their barstools, not wanting to even think about that. Their wives never knew why their menfolk came home at times all lovey-dovey, and they didn't care either. It made a pleasant change from just 'Where's my dinner?' even if the meal did get cold!

The small Bay of Plenty town had around six thousand people. The rush times of logging and the busy sawmill had become a trickle making many families move on to seek work elsewhere. There were more retired folk nowadays. Many from that big metropolis – Auckland, living well after selling their home for a goodly sum and buying cheap in the country. A new car and often a campervan, as well as the odd overseas trip, all part of the parcel. The local RSA did well from the 'newbies', as did the pubs and cafes. Most of the newcomers were great at volunteering too. You name it, they got involved. The old folk's home, the drop-in centre, the Red Cross, St. Johns. The new residents were caring people and warmly welcomed by the locals.

Ellen Carter, a widow in her early fifties, and her two daughters Carrie and Frith were among the latest newcomers to arrive. Carrie had been a medical receptionist in Auckland and quickly got a job doing just that. Frith was a hairdresser and with her mum's help, took on an empty shop and opened her own hair salon – 'A Touch of Class'. Ellen was a great help in the salon but most importantly, with her background in accounting, she managed the salon's finances. Ellen bought a roomy bungalow near the outskirts of town and began to plan changes, though for now, work was more important.

Ellen was a smartly-dressed, petite woman in her early fifties and the girls were definitely head-turners. One fair, the other dark haired, though thanks to Frith one never knew what colour streaks would be added each month. Polite, level-headed girls as brought up by their mum.

At the pub and the RSA, the talk among the men was how long it would be before big Billy made a move on the girls. One of the guys laughingly suggested taking bets on how long this would take. They didn't have long to wait.

On a lovely summer's Saturday evening Ellen, Carrie and Frith decided to try a pub meal, where you could eat outside and enjoy the cooling breeze.

As they waited at the bar to place their meal orders, Billy Buxton arrived. The locals watched, some nudging each other, as like a moth to a flame Billy approached the ladies.

He stood for a moment giving them the full force of his long-lashed, baby blue eyes.

"Good evening ladies, Billy's the name, Billy Buxton. Chippy and odd job man. You must be the folk that bought Palmers' old house. Know it well, I do. Done a bit of work on it over the years, so if you're planning any alterations I'd be glad to help." Billy smiled in what he considered a charming and friendly manner. "Are you staying to eat? I can recommend the steak, and the fish is always fresh. Joan in the kitchen is a great cook. Shame she's married and not single like me." He chuckled. "Well, enjoy your meals, ladies."

Happy with his initial move, he took his beer and joined the men at the leaners. The women wouldn't have been at all impressed to hear Billy boast, "Well that's the first contact, but it won't be the last I tell you. Here's to new conquests." He raised his glass in salute.

As they ate their meal Ellen and the girls discussed the big brawny man.

"A bit pushy I thought," said Ellen.

"Did you see the big boots he wore?" Carrie asked.

"Given the size of his feet, they had to be big, silly," Frith told her.

They all looked at each other as Carrie said, "Well you know what they say about big feet!" They simultaneously burst into laughter.

"Seriously," Ellen said. "It's summer and look around, none of the other men are wearing heavy boots."

"Oh, Mum. Maybe he has funny feet, or smelly ones," Frith said.

"How about we change the subject?" Carrie suggested. "Not the best of subject for over dinner."

Ellen and Frith agreed and Billy Buxton was soon forgotten.

It was about a week later when Billy Buxton walked into Frith's hair salon and asked, "I wonder, do you cut men's hair? As you can see, I'm long overdue for a haircut."

"Yes I do," Frith told him. "If you don't mind waiting, I'll just pop this client under the dryer and then check the bookings. No time today I'm afraid, but I may be able to book you in for tomorrow. Take a seat please. I won't be long."

With an appointment organised Billy left the salon with a smile on his face. Second contact made!

At the RSA women's club monthly meeting, Ellen was enjoying a chat when Anne Wilson commented, "Saw Billy Buxton leaving your salon the other day Ellen. Perhaps you should be aware that the man has quite a reputation in town. As a womaniser that is. Mind you, I don't believe half of what I've heard, probably a lot of exaggeration. Nevertheless he talks about his conquests, and not in a very nice manner either. It may be a good idea to warn your daughters."

Ellen smiled. "Thanks for the warning Anne but my daughters are adults with good heads on their shoulders, not at all gullible. I'm sure they'd be more than a match for the Billy Buxtons of this world."

Over breakfast the next morning, Ellen mentioned Anne Wilson's warning.

"I've already heard that Mrs Wilson is the gossiping type," Frith said, "but I reckon we summed Billy Buxton up the first night he came over to us in the pub, didn't we Carrie? One of my clients told me he'd tried to get into the Army years ago and was turned down. Trouble with his feet, flat footed or something."

Just the mention of his feet had them laughing.

One Friday as Carrie left her work at the Health Clinic, she was surprised to see Billy Buxton.

"I've been waiting for you Carrie," he said. "Thought you might like a cooling drink after a week's hard work. You choose the place." He tilted his head questioningly waiting for Carrie's answer.

He looked surprised when Carrie told him, "Not for me thanks, I'm looking forward to getting home and having a quiet evening with Frith and Mum."

Next it was Frith's turn for his unwanted attention. She was locking up the salon one evening when Billy startled her by appearing and asking almost the same question. Frith didn't mess about. Billy received a very abrupt answer. "Not interested," she said, and left to get her car. Had she looked back she would have seen Billy's round face redden, and his teeth clench in anger.

"Bitch, both bloody bitches," he spat as he watched Frith walk away.

Billy walked to his normal drinking hole and settled in to numb his hurt pride. It wasn't long before he was mouthing off, bragging that the Carter girls had been push-overs. Easy meat and, quite tasty too! Some of the men at the leaner got up and left. There were times Billy went over the top with his talk about women. Even Billy's couple of boozing buddies looked uncomfortable.

In a small town, talk like Billy's can get repeated and exaggerated, and it wasn't long before Frith and Carrie became aware of what he had said. They were absolutely ropeable at Billy's bad-mouthing them. They knew their mum would be too if she ever found out. They hoped she wouldn't. They'd sort Billy Buxton out in their own way.

It was Frith who came up with a plan that sounded pretty good to both of them.

A few days later, Frith spotted Billy in the main street of town. She greeted him. "Hi there Billy, haven't seen you for a while. How are you?"

Billy hesitated at her unexpected friendliness. "Pretty busy with renovating the shop next to the stationers, still a lot to do there. Going to be a café, but if you ask me there's already enough of them in town. What about you, how's the salon going?"

"Really well, and talking of that, you look as if you're due for another cut. Pop in some time and I'll book you in." Looking at her watch Frith said, "Gosh, look at the time. I'd better get on, got Mum's shopping list to attend to. See you Billy."

Billy watched Frith walk away, studying the curves of her neat little bottom in her tight jeans, and breathed out heavily. Cor! That was a turn-up for the books, he thought, but what the hell, I'll get my hair cut and see what develops. Whistling, Billy lumbered off down the street.

Frith, like most hairdressers, was a right chatterbox, and Billy sat in the chair enjoying the attention.

"Billy, you know everything about this area," Frith began. "Carrie and I have heard about a place out of town somewhere, an old quarry that's got a really good swimming hole. It sounds like a great place for a picnic, especially in this hot weather. Do you know where it is?"

"Do I what?" Billy said with a grin. "Better than telling you, why don't I take you out there and show you? It's only about twenty K's out of town, but it is well off the beaten track."

"Would you? That'd be super. Of course Carrie would want to come too, but you could cope with the two of us, couldn't you?" Frith smiled warmly in the mirror at Billy and gently smoothed his hair.

Hardly able to believe his luck Billy stuttered a shaky reply. "You tell me when and I'll pick you girls up. A picnic it is. And I'll bring the drinks and glasses. Bubbly for you and Carrie?" Billy grinned when Frith nodded her agreement.

"Sunday morning about eleven, okay?" Frith asked. "See you then. Oh – in case you're interested, Carrie gives a brilliant massage."

For the rest of the working week Billy went about his work in a state of suppressed excitement, his mind working overtime as he pictured what could happen at the swimming hole. Mentally, he slowly undressed the girls and thought of what would follow. The picnic rug; he must put that in the wagon. And thinking of that, he'd

149

better give the wagon a good clean. Inside, and out too. Oh boy, he was about to score – big time!

Sunday morning promised another scorcher of a day, with only the odd tuft of cloud and very little breeze. A few minutes before eleven a smiling Billy arrived to collect Frith and Carrie, along with their picnic basket and tote bags. Billy spotted towels. Good, they did intend swimming.

"Morning Frith, Carrie," he greeted them. "Give me your gear and I'll pop it in the back. Room up front for both of you." Joining the girls he checked, "Belted up? Right, then let's be off. The last few K's we go through are part of an old forestry road. Gravel only, so it'll be a bit bumpy but I think you'll be pleasantly surprised when you see the swimming spot. There's been a bit of planting done over the years and some of the trees are now big enough for shade."

Billy was quiet for a while as the girls chatted to each other. Then he asked, "Didn't see your mum this morning, sleep in on Sunday's does she?"

Frith replied "No, not our Mum. She never wastes a minute. She's already gone out. I think a walk in the rose gardens, lunch and then a movie with a friend is planned."

"Good on her." Billy commented, then pointed out an area that used to be covered in pine trees. "See the gorse and blackberry all along the roadside on this last stretch. Good for nothing but goats now," and he laughed at his own joke.

The girls decided Billy was right. They thought the swimming hole and the surrounding grassy area great, almost like an oasis in the middle of nowhere. Billy turned the wagon and parked it under a tree. Leaving the keys in the ignition he said, "No need to worry about having cars nicked here! Right, I'll get the gear out and you girls pick a good place for us to sit in the shade."

"Okay," Frith agreed. "But I think we should leave the picnic basket in the car for now, where it's cool."

With the rug laid out and his chilly bin nearby Billy poured the girls a drink. His eyes bulged as Frith and Carrie removed their shorts and tops, to reveal bikinis which left very little to the imagination. They popped their clothes into their bags, and accepted a cold glass of bubbly from Billy.

"Aren't you having any?" Frith asked him.

"Beer's my drink." Billy said, as he reached into the chilly bin and took out a can. He gurgled down a long swallow then burped loudly. "Pardon ladies," he said with a grin.

"Aren't you going to get comfortable too?" Carrie asked. That was all the encouragement Billy needed.

The girls watched fascinated as he undid his bootlaces, and struggled to remove his boots. Then he peeled his socks off and they saw his feet for the very first time. In the glare of the sun they shone a translucent white like raw fish and looked just as soft. Pudgy and flat bottomed. Aha! Definitely flat feet. Not really made for walking! Billy stripped off his shirt and shorts leaving on view a pair of speedo-style swimming trunks, and leant back on his elbows to watch the girls' reactions. They both smiled broadly at Billy who took this as their approval.

"Now, what's this I hear about massages, Carrie?"

"I did bring my massage oil." Carrie told him. "Very special and very expensive, but I suppose I could use some on you. What do you think Frith?"

Billy's reaction to the girls was becoming very obvious, and they smiled at each other.

"You know you only massage on a clean body, Carrie." Frith reminded her.

Billy was on his feet in an instant. "I am a bit hot and sticky, why don't we all have a swim?"

"Good idea, but you go in first Billy." Carrie smiled. "Leave us to sort out our gear and check the picnic basket. We won't be long."

With that, Billy lumbered down to the water's edge and with the water up to his waist, dived in out of sight.

The girls wasted no time. They picked up their bags and with Frith holding Billy's sweaty boots well out from her body, raced to the wagon. Throwing everything in the back they leapt in. Within seconds Carrie had the vehicle started and took off, roaring along the track back towards the main road. Above the noisy motor they heard Billy's shouts, then they were out of ear-shot and breathed sighs of relief.

All the way back they re-lived Billy's predicament. It would be a long, long walk home. Tough going for a guy with tender feet. But serve the creep right for slandering them the way he had!

Their sides were sore from laughing as they pulled up at home. Frith got into her car following Carrie to Billy's house. Swapping their gear into Frith's car they left the wagon in Billy's driveway, keys in the ignition. Billy, they reckoned, had been given a jolly good lesson. Frith and Carrie wouldn't tell anyone about what had happened, and thought it most unlikely that Billy would either. He wouldn't want folk to know how the girls had got the better of him.

There is an old saying about everyone having an Achilles Heel. One could almost feel sorry for poor old Billy. He had to find out the hard way that he had two of them!

HOME SWEET HOME

The early morning sun creeping into the room woke Julie. She listened to the chorus of bird-calls, luxuriating in the knowledge of not having to get up early, and snuggled down under the covers again – bliss.

As usual, Julie's thoughts went to her children – not children at all given their ages, but what else do you call them? Anyway, they were not only adults but parents themselves and lived full and busy lives. There was Leanne, now a happily-married mother of two enjoying life in Perth. Too far away, and too costly, to just pop across the 'ditch' and visit on a whim. Then Francis. Settled down at last with a lovely wife. At least they had stayed in New Zealand, but still not close enough to just call in and maybe stay for a meal. From talking to friends, it seemed the spreading out of families around the world had become the norm these days.

Julie stretched and yawned. Oh bother, now I need the bathroom. Well, so much for a lie-in she thought, looking at the bedside clock and noting it was not yet seven. Putting on her dressing gown and slippers she left the bedroom.

Later on she walked back down the driveway, morning paper in hand, looking forward to the first cuppa of the day. Not a soul in sight and no sounds bar the birds, lovely. The gentle breeze was coming from the south west and brought with it a slight tinge of sulphur, a reminder that yes, she did live in Rotorua.

Julie took her cup of tea through to the sunroom and having read most of what she was interested in, began to go through the 'Properties for Sale' section. This was her biggest interest at present. When her dear James had passed away unexpectedly six years ago, Julie had decided that when she retired she would sell up and move. Make a fresh start by looking for a special place in the country. A little bit of land and just a small house would do. That time had come and Julie was ready to make major decisions.

For the past fifteen years she had worked in the hospitality industry, mostly in hotel reception, a real eye-opener to human behaviour! The idea of writing a book based on these experiences had occurred to her, so maybe now was the time to tackle this.

Finding no properties of interest in the paper, Julie had her breakfast, showered and dressed. Putting on her makeup she frowned a little, realising that she was beginning to show her age. Still, she told herself, when she smiled she dropped at least ten years. She giggled out loud at the thought of going around with a continuous silly grin on her face. Blonde hair and green eyes weren't too bad a combination she consoled herself, and she did still have a reasonably young-looking body. 'Be thankful for small mercies' her mother would have lectured her.

One thing Julie had decided. Not to tell the family of her plans yet in case they had disparaging comments to make. She began to write a wish list. Land. A hectare or two. A stream would be lovely. Some big trees, well away from the house. House in good condition with insulation, heating and plumbing up-to-date. A sunny aspect and good soil for a vegetable garden, and a few fruit trees would be nice. Then other things to check. The distance from town, and water supply. A council LIM report and getting a 'P' check for methamphetamine use. From what she had seen on the TV it was best to be sure on that! Then beaches – there had to be one not too far away.

Most important of all – to go north or south? North would be warmer, but some areas in the Bay of Plenty could be interesting, especially near beaches and if near the sea, possibly warmer than Rotorua.

One thing Julie was sure about. A dog. Years ago she and James had a big gentle Labrador called Annie. They had named her after the Gentle Annie Highway in the Hawkes Bay region where she had been bred. Next to James, Annie had been Julie's best friend. Another Lab like her for company would be just perfect.

Now, what to do first. Get a valuation on her house or look at properties? She made a quick decision. She would go driving and see first-hand just what was available.

Julie decided to head south. She recalled a lovely drive she and James made once, past Okere falls through forestry and on to Pongakawa. They had come out on the east coast road somewhere south of Matata and driven south to Whakatane. They had stopped to watch the ghostly grey plumes of smoke issuing from far-off White Island. Only one way to check out how good her memory was; and onto the internet she went.

The next day Julie packed a suitcase, and a chilly-bin of basic food supplies in case of motel stops. The family had been sent e-mails as to where she was going, saying she should still be contactable on her mobile or by text, if need be. After a quick word with the neighbour happy to take in her mail, she left in high spirits, looking forward to the trip.

Julie stopped at the local Caltex station for petrol, and the obliging attendant also checked the oil and water as well. Obviously very observant, he asked, "Do you realise your warrant of fitness is due next week?"

"I had forgotten, actually," she replied. "Thanks for noticing. Come to think of it, the car has been a bit reluctant to start lately so a check-over is a good idea." She gave him a cheery wave as she left and made a mental note to get a WOF booked when she got home.

The weather was perfect for travelling. A mild spring day, the rich blue sky streaked with fingers of high cloud. Julie sat back and began to relax. She took her time, taking in the scenery and keeping a look out for 'Property for Sale' signs – just in case. Occasionally she pulled well over to let the driver of a following vehicle pass.

The road wound through dense forestry as she remembered it, twisting and turning, flashing from bright light to gloomy and back to light again. Sometimes a wide rough driveway appeared but whether it was a forestry road or led to a house she couldn't always tell.

Finally leaving the forest behind, Julie came to the expansive farmland area of Pongakawa. She received a wave from a farmer driving a tractor, then just the occasional farmhouse and outbuildings were to be seen, with grazing animals the only other sign of life. Twenty minutes or so later a signpost loomed ahead. Sure enough it indicated Matata to the left and Whakatane to the right. 'Well done' Julie told herself. Turning onto the coast road she headed south. Traffic was light and Julie tootled along enjoying the drive. There! She had to pull in, for old times' sake. Sure enough, in the distance were the tell-tale pale plumes of White Island. Some things never changed.

Reading the blurb she'd printed out, it seemed as though the Whakatane township could be the next stop. She read that Whakatane east had a population of over 18,000 and as the major centre for the Eastern Bay of Plenty it would be interesting to have a good look around the town. Maybe even stop the night, depending on finding a decent place to stay.

Julie followed the sign indicating the 'Town Centre,' and spotting a car-park area pulled in and parked. She looked forward to stretching her legs. She didn't have far to walk before she found a Real Estate office, where a pleasant lady who introduced herself as Marion made her very welcome. Julie briefly outlined the type of property she was interested in and Marion went to get her boss.

The Real Estate agent, a John Carson, showed Julie photographs of the few country properties he had listed. When Julie mentioned staying overnight he promptly recommended the local pub. He told her they had unusual, motel-style accommodation around the back of the pub. Great meals and quiet during the week too. It was late afternoon now. If she preferred he could drive her around to view properties, say tomorrow morning? And so it was arranged.

Julie was made most welcome by the owners of the pub; Bill, and his wife Mary. A friendly first-name basis from the word go. Bill walked Julie around to the motel units. John Carson had been right about 'unusual'. The units were in the settler style, each with their own private veranda. They were really lovely, blending in with the era of the hotel. Bill unlocked one of the units and with a flourish, opened the door saying to Julie, "After you."

The unit was as lovely inside as out. In the living area a small dining table and two chairs were at one end next to a small kitchen. At the other end, two comfy-looking armchairs and a small settee were positioned for viewing the television, with a selection of magazines on a coffee table. Off the lounge a door led into a charming bedroom, dominated by a huge bed covered in a bright paisley bedspread, the rest of the room in soft muted colours. Julie looked at the en-suite and thought it immaculate. She was most impressed. "The unit's lovely, thank you. I'm sure I'll be most comfortable here."

With the paperwork done and her car parked nearer her unit, Julie was settled.

She was surprised to wake up more than an hour later. Good heavens, almost six o'clock. The bed had been too tempting to resist and beautifully soft. Time to freshen up. All tidy again, Julie picked up her purse, and locking the door behind her went to make enquiries about dinner.

"Hello there love," Mary's welcoming voice greeted her. "Had a bit of a rest have you? Thought you looked a little weary. Now, can I get you a drink? Come on through to the side bar, it's nice and cosy in there. Then I'll get you the menu, though you won't want to eat just yet I'm sure."

"Actually, a small gin and tonic would be lovely, thank you." Julie settled in an old but most comfortable armchair, and sat admiring the room. So many interesting items. Keepsakes from days gone by, she guessed, and wonderful old photographs; historic no doubt. Mary brought her drink across to her along with a menu and left her in peace. Julie perused the menu and was pleasantly surprised at the selection. The good old-fashioned roast chicken with five vegetables and home-made gravy sounded perfect, and if she had room for one, the desserts were very tempting. Julie sat back quite content. John Carson was right, this hotel appeared to be a gem.

By six-thirty a few people had arrived for a drink and Bill had taken over from Mary at the bar. Handing him her glass with a smile and a thank you, Julie went in search of the dining room.

"Oh, there you are Julie," said Mary. "Ready to order are you? My son's cooking tonight and he's a very good cook even if I do say so myself."

"Hello Mary love," came a deep male voice. Julie turned to look at a man whose body perfectly matched the voice. A big man, six-foot-plus and built solid as a rock, he seemed to fill the doorway. He was smiling broadly at Mary and she returned his smile.

Julie took in the freshly shaved face and twinkling blue eyes and found herself smiling too. Mary briefly introduced the newcomer as George, then took their orders and hurried off to the kitchen.

George ate regularly at the pub. "That way I get two decent meals a week at least," he told Julie. "Always here mid-week and on a Sunday. A pretty basic cook myself, though I get by."

It seemed natural for George and Julie to share a table and Julie enjoyed his light-hearted company. She got to learn more about the town, finding that like many rural areas there was a downturn, so there were a few empty shops. Still, George said, tourism seemed to be on the rise and would certainly help. He lived a bit out of town himself and would be happy to show Julie around, that is, if she was interested?

Julie saw George frown and wondered why. He seemed to be watching a man who had arrived and sat eyeing the menu. A bit of a scruff, Julie thought. Dark lank hair, worn sneakers and unshaven, he sported tats on both arms. Mind you, so did many people these days. She sharply reminded herself not to be so judgmental. The man turned to stare at Julie, making her feel somewhat uncomfortable.

George made general conversation as if aware of her discomfort, and soon had her laughing at a local yarn that no doubt had grown in the telling. Julie found him good company. The meal was excellent and both of them did it justice, even managing a dessert, as well as a glass of wine. They then decided to meet up the next day at a local café for a light lunch and coffee – great.

Julie left first, saying goodnight to both Mary and George, and walked around the back of the pub to her unit. She fumbled in her purse for the unit key and unlocked the door. Opening the door, she was knocked forward by a rough shove from behind, and fell, landing hard. Then it seemed as if all hell had broken loose. She looked up to see George tussling with a man, the scruffy man from the dining room. He yelled as George knocked him down and sat astride him, twisting the man's arms up behind his back.

"Get off me, you f...... bastard," he shouted at George.

George ignored him. "Dial 111 Julie. I'll hold him till the local copper gets here."

Julie managed to stand, and though wobbly on her feet she made the call.

"Thought you had it made didn't you, you bloody creep," George told the guy squirming beneath him. "I was pretty sure I knew you when you came in for a meal. Coppers are trained to have good memories. I may be retired, but I never forget a face. You were a fool to come back to this town, but you won't be staying long. I had you put away once, now you'll be going back inside for sure."

The sound of a police car siren got louder and louder then stopped. Heavy footsteps followed and a uniformed policeman entered. Julie gave a sigh of relief.

The copper took one look at George and said, "What the hell George, what have we here? Thought you'd retired." He chuckled. "Life getting too dull for you mate?"

Mary and Bill came rushing in.

"Bloody Nora!" said Bill. "What the hell's happened here?"

Mary put her arms around a shaking Julie.

Julie sat down on a chair and held the side of her head that throbbed from where she had landed on the floor. She was so very relieved that George had been there.

"But if you knew him to be a problem, why didn't you stop him or at least tell me to look out for him?" she asked.

"Sorry about that, girl," he replied. "But I had to catch him in the act. Once a copper, always a copper, and I know the rules. You have to catch them in the act or nothing sticks. Proof, you always need proof. Anyway, how's your poor head lass? Nasty fall you took. Do you think you need a doctor?"

Julie said a definite "No."

George grinned at her as the handcuffed man was taken away for a night in the local lockup. "Shall I make you a cup of tea or coffee? Have you got any pain-killers for that head?"

"Stop fussing George," Mary told him. "I'll see to Julie. Go home and leave the poor girl in peace."

It was an exhausted Julie who finally got into bed. After making sure she had taken a couple of Panadol, Mary tucked her up in a motherly fashion. She put the snib door lock on as she left.

"I'll come and check on you in the morning Julie. Now do try and get some sleep. Goodnight, dear."

Surprisingly, Julie slept well and in the morning lay in the comfy bed pondering over the happenings of the night before. Wasn't she lucky George had been there? He was a nice man. She smiled, recalling that they were meeting for lunch later that day. She was looking forward to that. Eventually she rose and made herself a welcome coffee. A shower and then breakfast at the pub; not that she would eat much, not after that big dinner last night.

It was a relieved Mary who greeted Julie, giving her a gentle hug as she entered the dining room. "Hello love, I was just coming to check on you. Thought you would have stayed in bed this morning. Are you feeling okay after that awful time last night? Thank heavens George was here and remembered him." She fussed over Julie, guiding her to a seat where the sun streamed in the window. "Weather's lovely again, that's something. I'll get you a cuppa love while you decide what you want for breakfast. Now, tea or coffee?"

Julie sat, hands wrapped around a mug of lovely hot coffee, sorting out in her mind what she needed to do after breakfast. First she should check her texts. Then she wanted to drive around town and find a chemist to buy some more Panadol. Her head was still bothering her. Then she would be looking at properties with John Carson before meeting George for lunch.

After breakfast, Julie got into her car, put on the seatbelt and turned the key. Nothing. She tried again, nothing. She sat for a couple of minutes before she tried again. Just the lightest of clicks. Dammit, the car just wouldn't start. She belonged to the AA but would they have an agent in town, she wondered. One last try and Julie gave up, going to look for Mary or Bill.

"Oh yes, Julie," Bill assured her. "Frank Williams – he's the AA agent. Probably a battery problem or dirty spark plugs; something simple. Just ring the AA number on your membership card. They'll check your details and get a message to him straight away."

Within fifteen minutes Frank Williams was there, his head under the car bonnet. Julie waited. It wasn't just the battery – a part was needed. Frank didn't think he had one in stock, would have to track it down. If he could find one, getting it usually took overnight. He offered Julie a lift into town, as he had to pick up his tow-truck to take her car to his garage. She gratefully accepted the ride. Arriving in town, Frank wrote down Julie's mobile number saying, "Ring you later," and with that, she had to be satisfied.

The drive around with John Carson wasn't very productive. There were only three places that might have interested her and all fell well short of her 'wish list'. She looked forward to meeting up with George for lunch, feeling she could talk to him and get his thoughts on what she should do next.

Their chat was interesting, to say the least. Firstly, the car. George said Frank Williams did a good job and could be relied on to get her car running again. He was honest too and didn't charge an arm and a leg. "Actually," he added, "I'm rather pleased you'll be staying another night. Perhaps we could have dinner in town tonight, or at the pub again if you'd prefer. As my guest of course, what do you think?"

Julie looked at this nice, caring man, at his hopeful expression, and without a second thought said, "Yes. That would be lovely. I enjoyed your company last night, that is; all except the last bit." They both burst out laughing.

The day was full of surprises, the last and best one being taken to see George's 'wee' property, as he called it. Now if that had been on the market she would have snapped it up. A little piece of heaven, she thought, as they turned in at the end of a long tree-lined driveway. Julie sat admiring the quaint cottage nestled in against a backdrop of native trees and bush.

George smiled proudly. "There she is, Home Sweet Home."

There was a loud barking and from the side of the house bounded a soaking wet, solid looking, glossy black Labrador; tail going nineteen-to-the-dozen and tongue lolling with excitement.

Looking concerned George said, "He's been in the stream again, the blighter. I hope you don't mind dogs Julie. I guess I should've mentioned before, this is my best mate Jasper." He turned to see Julie's reaction but was too late. She'd already got out of the car and was now fussing over the big Lab who shook and sprinkled her with water. Julie just laughed.

Lucky dog, George reckoned with a grin. Funny the way things turn out. Perhaps Julie's car breaking down was meant to be and maybe between us, Jasper and I could encourage Julie to stay even longer. Looking at a happy Jasper and a delighted Julie, he certainly hoped so!

SLIPPERY SLOPES

Yahoo!

The College grounds resounded with loud cheers from a group of over-excited, unruly youths.

The only semblance of uniformity was the school uniforms, and now the boys were yanking out their shirt-tails and opening the top buttons to expose either hirsute chests, or almost bare ones.

No more rules, no more regulations. Or so they all thought. Schooling finished, not just for the year but for good. Sixteen years of age and pumped full of testosterone, they clapped each other's backs as they left the college grounds. A year to remember, nineteen fifty-six!

There were three boys who walked off together, already planning the next day and the next. The tallest of the trio, Joe, summed up their feelings.

"Bloody great," he said. "Freedom at last. What say we meet down at the beach? Cool off a bit and chill out."

Buster, a good nick-name for an overweight lad, was the first to agree, and the runt of the group, Shorty of course, joined in.

Grinning, Shorty said, "You're on. And I'll see if I can swipe a bottle of beer too. Dad won't miss just the one."

All sorted, the boys headed home.

It was going on five o'clock when they arrived at Island Bay. They wheeled their bicycles along the grass and finding a shady spot, lay back and talked. Plenty to think about, but no hurry. Except…

"Wouldn't you know it?" Joe began. "As soon as I got home Mum was onto me. 'Don't think you can just sit around now that you've finished school,' she told me. 'You need to get a job. I don't want you under my feet all day'." Looking glum he added. "She reckons the old man can get me a job at his work. Last bloody thing I want, working at Chelsea Refinery with him all day. Shit!"

Buster chimed in. "At least your mum cares. Mine doesn't give a damn what I do, as long as she doesn't know about it. And I wish I had a father to work with. You don't know how lucky you are."

They both looked at Shorty, knowing he would come up with something special – as usual. He took after his father who was an accountant. The academic of the group, his brain more than made up for his lack of height.

Shorty enjoyed making them wait. "I'll check the newspapers and see what's available. But not until late January. I gather no-one hires early in the year." He gave a contented sigh. "Until then I shall enjoy each day, doing bugger all."

Laughter accompanied his last comment.

Along the beach a group of teenage girls came into view. This had the lads sitting up to get a better look as they came closer.

"Cor," Joe muttered. "That's Julie, Briar and Samantha. Look different out of school uniform, eh?"

"Well stacked, that Briar. Right handful if you ask me," Buster said.

"Well, we didn't," Shorty told him. "But I must say they all appear rather delicious. Like peaches ready for picking."

As if tuning in to each other the three lads stood up, took off their sunglasses and began to casually saunter down to the water's edge, towards the floating punt.

"Hi there," came a chorus from the girls as they drew closer.

Acting surprised, the lads turned towards them.

"Oh, hi there," Shorty said. "Didn't see you."

Joe and Buster acknowledged the girls. "Are you here for a swim too?" Joe asked.

Before they could answer Buster said, "We were just going to swim out to the punt, want to join us? Toss your towels down with our gear. Come on, race you out there."

For a heavy lad Buster was a darned good swimmer, and was the first to heave himself up onto the punt, reaching down to give Briar a hand up.

All six of them sat, feet dangling in the beautifully cool water; quiet for a while. Then the chatting began. Mostly about school and what their plans were now. It was Shorty who mentioned the movie that was playing at the bug-house, this being the locals' name for the Birkenhead movie theatre.

"A really good murder, one of Hitchcock's," he said. "How would you girls like to go there on Saturday night? Our shout," he added, ignoring the horrified look on his mates' faces.

The girls looked at each other and Samantha, the tallest of the three, spoke for all of them. "We'd have to think about that and check with our folks first." Her friends nodded in agreement. "Give us a ring later."

An hour or so later they all swam back to the beach and having towelled themselves dry, started off home.

"Talk soon," Shorty said.

"Yeah, thanks. Will do," Briar acknowledged.

As the girls left ahead of them, Buster and Joe gave Shorty a wallop around the head. "What the hell were you doing asking them out like that?" Joe said.

"Yeah," Buster joined in "Really landed us in the crap haven't you? How are we getting there and getting them home? I'm flat broke so I'd have to ask Mum for money, and she's not likely to cough up any."

"Leave it to me," Shorty said. "I bet Dad will let me borrow his car and stump up with the cash for all of us to get to the movie, including the girls. Time you guys learned to live a little."

The upshot of the phone calls was Shorty picking up and cramming the entire group into his old man's roomy Ford V8 station wagon.

This first outing led to many others. It was odd how they paired off. The runt of the group, talkative Shorty, matched up with Samantha, the rather aloof tall brunette. But they tuned in on a mind level, each knowing just what they wanted from life and enjoying challenging discussions.

The original attraction Buster felt for the curvy red-headed Briar remained, and seemed to be reciprocated.

That left tall 'Mr. Smooth' Joe to become the protector of Julie, petite, blonde and seemingly helpless.

It was in the years of set expectations. Double standards in some ways. Males could, and did, sow their wild oats. Females were put into categories. There were the nice girls you were proud to be seen with, and that

170

your Mum would have approved of. Then the girls that provided the knowledge and teaching of sex. Definitely not marriage material let alone go steady with. Hypocritical – oh yes.

And so at times, relationships were strained for the six good friends. The boys openly discussed these frustrations among themselves. The girls only went as far as to tell each other, 'he tries' and embarrassed, said no more.

Years later the girls found out that the boys all lost their virginity to one particular girl. According to the boys she was a willing teacher and enjoyed sex every bit as much as they did. In retrospect the girls thought she had done them all a favour!

It was the era of the popular author Barry Crump's books, and with all three lads keen hunters, a lot of time was spent in the bush up in the hills at Puhoi, north of Auckland. The other attraction there was the beaut pub. The publican of the time turned a blind eye to his customers' ages. As long as they behaved themselves, the young chaps were welcome to drink in his pub, and this they did after a day's shooting. Sometimes they got nothing or if lucky, potted the odd rabbit or better still, wild goat. Gutted and taken home for the poor mum to cook, it did made a good stew or curry.

It was a wonder they even got that far in the cars they drove – old Holdens and Fords that kept the lads poor. They were lucky that Joe's dad had a work pit in his garage. Even had a block and tackle set-up, and many hours were spent replacing parts to keep the cars running. The Ford that Joe drove had a habit of boiling over if he went over fifty miles per hour. You never travelled without a container of water and a can of petrol, as there weren't many petrol stations back then. Even tyres were a constant expense. New ones were out of the question, most being bought at the wreckers in Albany, same as any parts that were needed. Still, between them there was always at least one car in a driveable condition.

The girls had settled into work. Joe's – Julie, as a clerk in a solicitors' office. Buster's – Briar, was training to be a hair-dresser and Shorty's – Samantha, loved her job at the local vets.

The lads were also achieving their aims. Joe, always outgoing, went into tourism. As a salesman he proved especially popular with the ladies. Buster was taken on as an apprentice in the building trade. Trimmed down too with all the hard yakker. Shorty had finally decided on becoming a teacher, and was now in his last year at Teachers' Training College.

But they still got together regular as clockwork. The Three Musketeers, Shorty reckoned. 'One for all and all for one.'

There was plenty to do of a weekend, quite apart from fixing cars! There was Speedway and Stock-cars at Western Springs. In the summer, always the beach. Swimming and barbecues. Movies of course, and the occasional party when their folks went away for a day or two.

The girls got their way sometimes, the boys taking them to dances at the local Beach Haven hall. Thank goodness for Rock & Roll they thought, as the boys were useless at 'proper' dancing. No alcohol was allowed at the dances and they knew the boys stashed a bit of booze in the shrubbery at the back of the hall. Their going out 'for a leak' was a frequent occurrence, which the girls chose to ignore.

The years flew by and two of the couples got engaged; the age of twenty-one being seen as the 'norm' in those days.

Joe and Julie though, made no such commitment. Joe seemed to be enjoying life to the full and told his mates, "I've no intention of getting tied down yet, and no need either," he would say with a nod and a wink. Quiet Julie just went along with whatever Joe wanted.

The change came about slowly, one could say insidiously.

The indications were there if you'd looked for them. Joe had bought a newer car and so it was Joe that became the number one driver. With the car came a change in Joe too. His hair slicked back in the latest style, wearing the latest clothes and even smelling, as his mates told him, 'Like a bloody pansy.' Joe was turning into a loud-mouthed pain. Showing off in front of the girls, bragging about the big money he was now earning, always out to impress. This began to put a strain on all their relationships.

With the arrival of spring, the guys began to plan a day's shooting. Up at Puhoi of course. Time to get out the rifles and give them a good clean. They all had .22 rifles and as well, Joe had recently bought a .303 rifle and was really keen to try it out.

The Army Surplus store was like an Aladdin's cave for campers and hunters alike, with really good prices. That's where Joe went to buy camouflage clothing, a cap and an ammunition belt for his new rifle.

It was before dawn when he arrived to pick up Buster and Shorty. Grinning, Buster asked, "When's the war starting Joe?" and he and Shorty roared with laughter.

"Well, at least I won't scare off any animals. Not like you stupid 'idjits' crashing around in your bloody bright red Swanndris and caps." Joe retorted. And with that they were on their way, Joe's foot rather heavy on the accelerator. Buster and Shorty raised their eyebrows at each other. Looked like they were in for a quick trip!

Glenfield, Albany, and Orewa all flashed by. Then it was over the bridge at Waiwera and on up the winding hill. Coming down, the road finally levelled out and on the left a faded sign signalled PUHOI.

As dawn began to break, they drove through the village and on past the pub to old man Walter's farm. From here they would start their tramp up into the heavily forested hills.

As Joe pulled up the farmer appeared from behind the woodshed. "Gidday fellas, heard the car. Cor, look at this. Getting paid too much are you Joe? Hope you've got some canvas or such in the back. Don't want blood and guts all over that posh wagon, do you?"

Not waiting for Joe's reply he turned away, saying, "Good hunting lads, and watch yourselves. We've had a fair bit of rain overnight. Could be a mite slippery on those hills." And he headed for the house.

With packs on their backs and rifles in hand the lads headed off. After crossing the flats they forded the shallow toe-toe-edged creek and tramped on towards the mostly manuka scrub. There was not a rabbit to be seen. After about an hour's trekking, the contour of the land changed as they entered the dark, heavily wooded, hilly forest. Above them mature puriri, totara and rimu towered. No one talked now, as the going got harder and they listened in hope for sounds of goats.

It was a good hour later when, reaching a grove of giant kauri, Joe stopped. "Time for a breather, don't you reckon?"

"We can't stop now," Shorty said. "We're not high enough yet. We need to keep going for at least another hour if we're going to spot any goats."

"Tired are you Joe? Late night last night was it?" Buster chimed in rather sarcastically.

Joe glared at them. "Look, if you guys are in a hurry, bugger off. I just need a breather. I'll catch up with you in a few minutes."

Shorty and Buster looked at each other and shrugged. The fact was, they were getting brassed-off with Joe and his moods. "Okay then," Buster said, and with a nod of agreement from Shorty, they moved on up the track and out of sight.

Left on his own, Joe's pent-up emotions grew stronger and stronger. It didn't matter how much money he made. Even the new car. Nothing made up for the one thing he wanted most in the world – Samantha. All these years he had wanted her, loved her; so much it hurt. It was unfair. Samantha should be his. Anger flared and there was no room for logic. His growing hate for Shorty, spawned from jealousy, finally consumed him.

He recalled old man Walter's warning, 'The hills could be slippery under foot.' The old bugger could be right. Accidents can happen on wet and slippery ground!

Joe rose to his feet, and with a bitter grimace, lovingly caressed the shiny wooden butt of his beautiful new rifle. His hands were steady, his mind calm as he loaded the magazine and slotted it back in place. He was an excellent shot. He knew one would be enough.

He hurried on up the winding track to catch up with his mates, eager to sight his prey, eager to make a kill.

FAMILY FUN

Miss Wilson called out, "Quiet, children, quiet."

As if by magic the room fell silent. The children knew they ignored their teacher at their peril, knew from experience, to be obedient.

Miss Wilson was a spinster for whom teaching had become the centre of her otherwise rather dull life. She lived in a small cottage close to town with her cat Baxter, the only male company she enjoyed.

A tiny woman, barely five foot tall, with dark clothes hanging on her thin breastless frame, she faced her class, cane in hand. Fair hair pulled harshly back into a bun at the nape of her neck served only to enhance her severe appearance. Little wonder her class of eight-year-olds sat in silence as told.

"This morning," she began, "we will learn all about the man 'Guy Fawkes'. Who he really was, what he did, and why you children are saving your pennies to buy fireworks ready for the 5th of November. This is true English history. A real event in exciting times of plots and rebellion."

Her class sat up straight, eager to hear more. Miss Wilson might be strict but she could be jolly interesting too.

After school Janet walked home with her best friend Nancy. The girls were different, beginning with their looks. Nancy brown-eyed with dark hair kept in thick shiny plaits. She was rather on the chubby side like her mum. Janet, fair-haired and blue-eyed with short hair, had not a spare ounce of fat to be seen. And, Janet had only sisters, Nancy only brothers. Janet was glad she didn't have any brothers. She found Nancy's brothers noisy, smelly and rough – ugh! No wonder Nancy preferred to come to her place to play.

"I'm glad that man Fawkes tried to blow up those buildings," Janet said. "Cause if he hadn't we wouldn't have Guy Fawkes' night, would we?"

"No," Nancy agreed. "And we wouldn't have a bonfire or a late supper, with all the family there, including Grandma and Grandpa."

"You forgot the most important part – the fireworks," Janet reminded her.

"No I didn't, I didn't forget. I just left the best bit till last," Nancy answered with a toss of her plaits. "I'm still saving up to buy fireworks, but my oldest brother Chad said he'll buy me some fireworks too. He's got money now he's working, so I'm lucky."

Not to be outdone Janet said, "My eldest sister Pam's the same. She's got a super job typing, and Mum says she gets good money too. Pam's going to buy fireworks from Mr. Doo. He's a Chinaman who has a big shop in the city, and he has the best fireworks ever."

Arriving at Nancy's place, the girls said their goodbyes and Janet hurried on home.

As she went in the front door, Janet smelled the delicious aroma of cooking. Whoopee! Her favourite. Tripe and onions with bacon for dinner tonight, with heaps of mashed spuds and Dad's peas from the garden – yum. Mum is a smashing cook, she thought. She dropped her schoolbag onto her bed and followed her nose to the kitchen. "Hi Mum. I'm home," she said, burrowing her head into her mum and getting a big warm cuddle in return.

"Thought I heard you come in. Did you have a good day love?" her mum asked, as she began to get Janet a cold drink and a couple of homemade ginger biscuits.

Janet told her all about the things she had learned that day, and how she'd learned why they had a Guy Fawkes' night.

"Good girl," her mum said. "You have listened well. I guess what that man did was very wrong, but I must say the way politicians go on I'm not surprised it happened, not surprised at all. Now, you best get changed out of those school clothes and bring out your homework. I'm sure you've got some. No going out to play until it's done."

That evening, Beverly Mason told her husband Peter of the lessons Janet had learnt that day, and how excited the child was waiting for Guy Fawkes' night.

A couple of weeks later on a Saturday morning, Janet sat on her bed. She opened an old shoe-box and gloated over its contents. With her pocket money she had been gradually buying fireworks. One by one she removed them from the box, saying their names out loud as she took them out. Silver Rain, Golden Glow, Flower Pot, Roman Candle, Rainbow Fountain, Catherine Wheels, and a packet of Sparklers. Sparklers were great fun. All the family liked holding them and waving them around and around. She sniffed the lovely smell that only fireworks had. Oh, yes, she bubbled with excitement. Only one more week to go!

Putting the treasured fireworks away, she slid the box back under her bed. She wondered what fireworks Nancy had.

"I'm going to Nancy's, Mum," she called as she left the house.

Walking in the open back door she greeted Nancy's mum politely. "Hello Mrs. Bates, is Nancy home?"

"Hello Janet. Yes, love, she's in her room I think, not long been up. Mind you, we all try and have a bit of a sleep-in on Saturdays."

"We do too." Janet nodded, and went to find Nancy.

The girls went through Nancy's collection of fireworks. Nearly as many as Janet had. Both of the girls talked of getting more from their parents as well as the ones from their elder siblings. Janet had asked especially for some Jumping Jacks. They were great fun. What a super night it would be. They listened to Nancy's noisy brothers. Nancy raised her eyebrows at Janet saying, "Blooming brothers; let's go to the park."

The night before Guy Fawkes Janet could hardly sleep. It felt a bit like Christmas Eve, the waiting. She hoped it would be a fine night for Guy Fawkes.

Beverly Mason had food ready for supper. In the back garden a couple of chairs had been put out for the 'oldies' to sit on, and Peter had put a large offcut of a tree stump in a prominent position for the placing of fireworks.

He'd also left a bucket of water handy – just in case it was needed – hopefully not. Then he made sure there was a clear section of fence for attaching Catherine Wheels, putting the hammer and nails nearby. Catherine Wheels were Gran's favourite. Peter was always well organised and on Guy Fawkes' Night he was the one in charge.

Beverly had been heard to say, 'Giving orders just like he's still in the Army'!

Janet's stomach was doing flips with the excitement of it all. The shoe-box was nearly full and as well as her eldest sister Pam buying some fireworks, her Dad had bought some too. It should be a smashing show.

The day dawned fine; what a relief. After all it was spring, often wet one minute and sunny the next. At school, Guy Fawkes' Night was all the children talked about.

That day Miss Wilson found her pupils rather more difficult to handle. Over-excited, in her opinion. She would have to bring poor old Baxter indoors early, so he wouldn't get too frightened with all the whooshes, screams and bangs. Not a good time for animals, she tutted. Thank heavens it was only once a year.

As the bell rang for home time, she addressed her class. "Now children, what is the most important thing to remember tonight?"

The children chorused 'Stay safe' and 'be careful'.

"And don't forget your pets," Miss Wilson told them. "Make sure they are safe. They get frightened you know and may run away."

With a 'Yes, Miss Wilson' the children scrambled to leave the class.

When Janet got home she was chuffed to find her mum had bought some Jumping Jacks. Never knowing which way they would go once lit and on the ground kept everyone on their toes; part of the fun.

After dinner was finished and her older sisters had done the dishes, Janet knelt on a chair, her elbows on the wide kitchen windowsill. With her head half out the window she waited impatiently for the dark of night to come.

"Watching won't make it get dark any quicker you know," Beverly told her pent-up daughter. "Come and help me butter some fruit loaf and get out the iced buns for supper; and ginger-crunch too, I mustn't forget that. We'll all want a cuppa later on." Seeing Janet screw up her nose she added, "You miss, can have cocoa instead, alright?" Janet grinned and went to help her mother.

They had just finished laying out supper when a scream from a rocket pierced the air. Janet ran and put her head out the window. Yippee! She caught a glimpse of a rocket as it shot into the sky then with a loud bang, layers of red and silver stars trickled slowly to the ground.

"Look," Janet said, "It's getting really dark. Can we go outside now? Please Mum, please Dad." Her sisters and Gran and Gramps agreed with her, so they all trooped outside.

As the eldest girl, Pam always got the job of holding the torch for her dad. He placed a candle stub in a big old tin and lit it. This he'd use for lighting some of the fireworks. Better than matches, he reckoned.

With the sound of fireworks going off, the old German Shepherd dog next door started howling. Janet told them what Miss Wilson had said about looking after your pets.

"Just as well we don't have any to worry about then, isn't it?" her mum commented. Janet said nothing, as not being allowed to have a pet was to her, a great disappointment.

Gran and Gramps were settled in their chairs with warm rugs draped around their legs.

Everyone went quiet as the show began. Oohs! and Ahhs! were plentiful. Peter did a great job naming each firework before he lit them. The sky was set alight with colours, outlining the trees. It was magical. Then the Sparklers were handed out. Everyone waved them around and around, the girls dancing on the dewy grass. As one sparkler died down they lit another from the hot metal stubs.

Then their mother joined in the fun of the evening, lighting and tossing a Jumping Jack Cracker across the lawn. It landed awfully near Peter, who jumped nervously. Then kept on jumping! Oh heavens. The well-named Jumping Jack had jumped into one of his trouser cuffs. Flicking his trouser leg Peter yelled, "Get the damn thing out." He who never ever swore! Watching their father leaping around caused laughter to spill out from all the girls. Even Gran and Gramps suppressed a smile, while the girls' Mum just looked guilty. Peter yelled again, and without a second thought Cathy picked up the bucket of water and tossed it over her father's trouser legs.

"What the blazes!"

The girls were quiet for a few minutes, avoiding looking at their father. By now there were only a few fireworks left. The old folks who had sat comfortably watching the show, still waited to see the Catherine Wheels spinning around on the fence. Rather grumpily, Peter obliged, dripping trousers and all.

Finally the show was over and everyone went indoors for supper. It was a rather subdued father who joined them, having changed into dry trousers. Eventually, accepting his wife's apology and seeing her rather mischievous grin, he too saw the funny side of the incident and joined in the family laughter.

The story was told and re-told over the years. Sons-in-law came into the family and ended up sharing the role of master of the show. Sadly, Gran and Gramps had long since passed away. Mum and Dad were now 'the oldies'. A new generation of children continued to enjoy the fun and with cuffs on trousers now out of fashion, there was no chance of hot–or wet–trousers!

These days, the 'Politically Correct' brigade are trying to stop the public sales of fireworks all together. Some folks, including the animal-loving Miss Wilsons of this world, agree. Others think going to watch a public fireworks display just isn't the same family fun and that's true too.

Perhaps, as in many areas of life, personal responsibility for one's actions is the answer. Now, what do you think?

FINALE

The final three works in this book form a separate unit.
Autobiographical in feeling though not always entirely
fact. They are a merest glimpse into my childhood.

EARLY BEGINNINGS

On the twenty-ninth of December 1873 the ship *Hindostan* arrived at the port of Auckland, in New Zealand. The voyage from London had taken a hundred and six days.

The passengers, both first class and immigrants, were mightily relieved to finally reach their destination. First class passengers were, of course, to be disembarked first. It was noted in the passenger shipping list that there were far more immigrants than paying passengers.

Among the immigrants listed were, from Kent, Cave-William John 33. Cave-Caroline Amelia 33. Cave-Henry James 4. Listed separately as a single man; their eldest son Cave-William John aged 13.

As they looked out from the ship, the town of Auckland presented a sorry sight to the new arrivals. Hardly any buildings of note to be seen; no cobbled streets and in the distance, bare hills with just the odd

185

building dotted here and there. A church of unknown denomination stood high on a hill – a reassuring sight of civilisation to many. The noise was overwhelming. Men shouted orders as cargo was unloaded, accompanied by the mournful sound of animals wanting to be free. Female passengers stood waiting to descend the gangway, perfumed kerchiefs held delicately to their nose to cover the rank smell of animals.

On the wharf, pick-pockets made the most of the unwary well-dressed first class passengers. Ladies of the night already strolled, parasol in hand, looking for customers, and of those there were plenty.

But how wonderful to finally be in New Zealand.

Twenty-six years later, on September 1899, a new child was to be born into the Cave family. In Auckland a steep street named College Hill led upwards away from the waterfront. On both sides of the street, really more of a muddy track than a street, small, wooden, square fronted bungalows huddled close together, verandas facing each other across the road.

In one of these humble buildings the aunt of Minnie Matilda, second wife of Henry James Cave, operated her midwifery business. Here, Minnie gave birth to her first child, a son. With arms full of soiled cloths, the aunt bustled out of the room. Minnie's mother stayed by her side. Minnie was soaked in perspiration from her efforts and lay exhausted but content, as she gazed down at the crying infant nestled against her breast.

"Thank you for staying with me Mother," she said, and smiled as she gently touched the infant's brow. "My beautiful boy, isn't he beautiful Mother?"

Her mother agreed. "Welcome to your new life little one, a new life in this new land." Then she hurried away to tell her son-in-law the good news.

Arriving at their house she followed sounds coming from the back yard and found him chopping wood for the stove. He paused, waiting for her to speak. "You have a son, Henry," she told him. His reaction to the news was brief and to the point. "And about damn time too," he said and without even asking after his wife and child, he continued on with his task.

The old woman shook her head in dismay as she muttered the words, "God help my poor girl," and returned to the house.

It had been no surprise to her the type of career that Henry had chosen. He was a Lieutenant in the Auckland Naval Garrison Volunteers, a position which suited Henry's authoritative nature admirably.

Before the hour was out, just in case the infant was taken by the Lord, a Minister of the Cloth had been sought to christen the infant – Wilfred Huia Cave. Pragmatic, but realistic as it needed to be.

His second name Huia was chosen by his mother Minnie as an example of his being treasured; the feathers of the native Huia bird being highly prized by Maori.

The child flourished and grew tall and strong.

Almost five years later – October 1904, in a bow-fronted villa in Chamberlain Street, Grey Lynn, a girl child loudly pronounced her arrival.

Along the hallway, in the parlour, her father stood; one hand resting on the solid kauri mantle-piece as he gazed into the glowing fire.

John had been musing over early memories. He had been born in Melbourne, Australia in 1870. His father was a Melbourne shipmaster whom he did not remember, as he had died when John was only a small boy. When John was eight years old his mother made the brave decision to cross the Tasman Sea to New Zealand. Arriving in Auckland they travelled by boat to settle in Thames and here a new home was made. To make a living, John's mother took in sewing, and found her skills in high demand. Thames may have had a reputation of lawlessness, but also of opportunity; with the gold found in both Thames and nearby Waihi.

Shortly after he finished school, John Freeman was suddenly left an orphan. He'd always hung around the wharves watching and admiring the boats and barges that berthed at the wharves. The attraction that ships held was strong, and as soon as he left school he applied for work at the local shipping office. This was to be the beginning of his career as a seaman.

Now he drew heavily on his pipe and listened with relief to the sound he had been waiting for. As a ship's captain he was not easily given to tears but they came unbidden. He was a father again. Thanks be to God. As he tapped out his pipe on the iron fireplace fender his mother-in-law entered the room, and smiling, announced the arrival of a healthy second daughter.

John hid his disappointment at the fact that he did not have a son and asked, "Is May well? Can I see her and the child now?"

"Shortly John, I shall call you soon," she said, and bustled away.

When John entered the room he smiled to see his wife sitting up radiant with satisfaction at the sight of her new child. He had always thought his wife beautiful, but never so much as at this moment.

He stooped to kiss her brow and gazing down at the wee bundle remarked, "Beautiful, like her Mother." May's face flushed a soft pink at his words and she took his hand saying, "I am sorry I have not given you a son this time my love. But there will be more children I am sure."

With this reassurance, John Freeman was content.

The infant, who was named Rose Margaret Maria, grew into an inquisitive child, seeking and asking for answers on all manner of things to the exhaustion at times of her parents and her older sister Dorothy.

It was only eighteen months later that the family in Chamberlain Street welcomed another infant. Again a girl, christened Rene, and John, unwilling to put his wife through any more suffering, said this child was to be the last. After all, he reasoned with May, once their three beautiful daughters were married he would have three ready-made sons. And so the small household settled into a comfortable life.

In 1913 John Freeman was promoted from 1st mate to Master of the *SS Taniwha*. This role as ship's Captain, or Skipper as his crew called him, took John away a great deal.

The steamship run from Auckland to Paeroa and Thames and back could take up to a week. Captain Freeman would regale his wife and daughters with tales of fog along the Waihou River. He could tell just how close the ship came to the banks by ringing the ships bell regularly and listening for the sound of the returning echo. Always racing the tide, and needing to keep a sharp eye out for snags in the fast running river.

He spoke of gold shipments from the Martha gold mine in Waihi, destined for Auckland, stowed away under the bunk in his cabin. For this reason he slept lightly, always alert, with a pistol under his pillow.

Cargo carried varied from household supplies to timber, coal, kerosene, and even prized race-horses. Captain Freeman spoke of the passengers they carried, politicians and famous opera stars – including Dame Nellie Melba-among them. 'We put out the red carpet for her,' he told the family.

Before the wharf was built at the Ohinemuri junction, the steamers had to go to the town wharf at Paeroa. To do this they had to go through two drawbridges while going up the river. One near Kopu and the other three miles south of there. If the bridge-keeper went to sleep while on duty, this was a problem for the Skipper. In a log-book of Captain Freeman's it was recorded, 'Nearly blew the top off the siren trying to wake the keeper!'

His daughters would listen wide-eyed to their father's tales.

Of course he never told them of the gamblers who regularly travelled the river, and the women – definitely not ladies, who often accompanied them.

During his frequent absences the role of parenting fell heavily on May. Perhaps this sense of responsibility caused her to become rather a martinet with her children, or maybe she was frightened of letting John down; who knows? Whatever the reason the girls learned to behave as young ladies should; any misdemeanours being settled in a most unpleasant way.

To one side of the backyard, near to the house, were two adjoined solid wooden sheds. There were no windows, just a door on each for access. One side was the wood-shed, the other a coal-shed. Both were used frequently for the wood-burning kitchen stove and the fireplaces in the sitting room and parlour.

In the darkest and dirtiest shed punishment was carried out. The offending child would be locked in the coal-shed, in with the spider webs and spiders, with only room to stand and barely able to turn around. The girls had found that after a while your eyes adjusted, and you could just see a crack of light at the bottom of the door. They all agreed that if you kept an eye on that and recited poetry, you could stay calm until mother came to let you out. Little wonder that they became very well-behaved children!

Rose was the only daughter to challenge her parents' expectations of her. This was to become a well-educated and elegant hostess, proficient in needlework and music. Be courted, marry well and eventually become mistress of her own home. Apart from piano lessons this did not suit Rose! She excelled at school and told her parents that she aimed to work in the legal field. Her parents were horrified. Their daughters had no need to work, and why wasn't Rose like her sisters, both of whom were quite happy to conform to their wishes?

But Rose never gave in, and eventually her parents conceded. Aged sixteen she finished her schooling with excellent results, and was accepted by a firm of barristers and solicitors to train as a conveyancing clerk. She loved the independence, the new friendships she made, and enjoyed the daily tram rides to and from her work in Queen Street. Rose Freeman had found her niche.

The boy child Wilfred Huia Cave grew up to be part of a small family. It would be another five years before his sister Ruve was born. Wilfred however, remained closest to his mother. A sensitive lad, he was only too well aware of the way in which his father treated his mother.

Minnie and the children came to dread the alcoholic binges to which Henry periodically succumbed, for they were the ones who had to cope with the wild furious rages which beset Henry Cave.

A move from Auckland to Gisborne was made. Here Henry went into partnership with his brother William, establishing The Cave Bros. Sawmill. The actual bush mill was at Te Karaka with the timber yard in the main street of Gisborne, next to the town's fire-bell.

After a few years, a falling out between Henry and his brother William necessitated a move back to Auckland for Henry, Minnie and the children.

Henry decided to buy a small farm north of Auckland. He found what he was looking for at Dome Valley, near Warkworth. Minnie was disappointed at the small farmhouse, but she would manage. The main thing was the land. Good fertile land. With a well near the house and a stream that ran freely, there would be no shortage of water. The hills were suitable for sheep, the flats for breeding beef cattle and a well fenced paddock took care of the horses. Henry planned on raising pigs as well. They would need to buy a house cow for milk and the making of butter, and of course some poultry. With a large vegetable garden and a small but productive orchard, the family expected to be self-sufficient.

Wilfred and his sister Ruve attended the Dome Valley Primary school and rode there, a distance of some five miles, tethering a horse on a loose rein alongside the other children's hacks. Wilfred much preferred school to home and quickly excelled at reading, writing, mathematics and geography. Books opened up new worlds for him. While immersed in a book, he was content. His teacher allowed him to take books from the school library home with him – with the ruling that they were to be treated with care. Wilfred burned many candles reading in his room at night. Even his mother said he was using far too many!

If it weren't for his father's mistreatment of his mother, Wilfred would have been content to stay on the farm. Only once, when in his early teens, did he challenge his father. A fist to the head was the result and his mother had begged him never to interfere again.

World War I broke out in 1914. In 1916 at barely sixteen years of age, Wilfred returned to Auckland where he boarded with an aunt in Ponsonby. He then studied for and gained his 1st class certificate as a wireless operator. With this qualification, he worked his passage to England. Like many young men in wartime, he had falsified his age and once in England he joined the Royal Engineers as a divisional signaller.

When the war was over Wilfred was back living with his aunt. Like most returned service men he never spoke much of his time in England and France. Now eighteen, he was a handsome young man, being tall and broad of shoulder – work on the farm and his time in the Army had seen to that. He spoke well and being an avid reader of newspapers, kept himself well informed. He found an advertisement for a sales agent in a Real Estate company intriguing; and obtained an interview. To his surprise he was readily accepted and a new future began.

The years flew by. Wilfred was now a mature man of twenty-two. He was in his element selling real estate. He had been supplied a motorcar, a magnificent 1917 soft-topped Buick Tourer D35, and he quickly learned how to drive. It soon became obvious that selling land and property was Wilfred's forte and he became quite the young man about town.

Having a strong dislike of his father's drinking habits, Wilfred seldom drank and planned his future carefully. He had saved a reasonable amount of money, enough he hoped, to soon be able to put the deposit down on a house.

And so in the thriving town of Auckland, Rose and Wilfred, two young people from very different backgrounds were destined to meet.

The skies were heavy with cloud and held the chilly damp that Auckland had in winter-time. Wilfred was driving home when he remembered that he needed cigarettes. He steered his car in to stop by the trading store on Richmond Road in Grey Lynn. Wilfred stepped down from the car, leaving the engine running rather than have to use the crank-handle to start the car again. Hearing the loud clanging bell of a tram he glanced back, and watched a young lady as she walked from the tram towards the store.

Wilfred was overcome by this vision of beauty. The girl, for he now saw she was very young; wore a rich red woollen coat with a soft white fur collar. Her hands were enclosed in a matching white fur muff. A small red feather brightened her hat, a jaunty black cloche, and sensible but dainty black boots kept her feet from the cold and damp.

All this he took in quickly as he discreetly tried to see more of her face.

As the young lady went to enter the store Wilfred stepped aside and, as a gentleman would, doffed his hat, indicating she precede him. He watched as she chose a mixture of boiled sweets, indicating her choice to the proprietor. Wilfred noted the girl's eyes were as green as emeralds, her skin pale with cheeks prettily flushed from the cold. The little hair he could see from beneath her hat shone a rich russet brown. A pert nose framed a mouth which reminded him of a tiny pink rosebud. Wilfred realised he was staring and quickly looked away. From her muff the lady produced a small coin purse, paid for her purchase and left the store.

Wilfred shook himself from his reverie and made his purchase of 'Players Navy Cut' cigarettes. Paying for these he asked, "May I enquire as to the name of the young lady?" Seeing the man frown he said, "I can assure you, my intentions are wholly honourable."

"The lady, sir, is one of the Freeman family. Miss Rose Freeman. Three daughters the Captain and his wife have, all beauties, if you'll pardon my comment. They live just down towards the bottom of Chamberlain Street. Well respected family they are."

Having made his purchase Wilfred thanked the man and wished him good day.

Wilfred was smitten. He could not stop thinking of the girl he had seen, and after a restless night had made up his mind. This was the girl he would marry. The girl with whom he would spend the rest of his life. Of this he had no doubts whatsoever.

He lost no time in finding the home of the Freeman family. After ascertaining that the little lady in black who answered the door was indeed Mrs. Freeman, he requested a meeting with her husband. As the Captain was away aboard ship at the time, it was several days later that the meeting with Captain Freeman took place. An anxious time of waiting for young Wilfred.

Finally the day came. In a forthright manner Wilfred stated his love for Rose, as he now knew her to be, and his request for courtship with the intention of marriage. John Freeman, being wary and most protective of all his daughters, grilled the young man thoroughly.

Finally satisfied with Wilfred's answers, John asked his wife to bring Rose in to meet him. When Rose entered the sitting room she was formally introduced to her hopeful suitor.

The blush of Rose's cheeks did not go un-noticed by her father. He sensed an immediate rapport between the young couple, and at his suggestion, May went to prepare afternoon tea.

As a result, a meeting of Wilfred's parents was sought. Only after this, would Wilfred's request to court Rose be considered. That is, if Rose also approved, and of this there seemed to be no doubt.

Both sets of parents met and agreed that the courtship could commence. Rose most definitely did approve and was delighted with Wilfred.

Within six months, with the blessings of their parents, an engagement was announced. At the end of another six months, on the tenth of April, 1923, the wedding of Rose and Wilfred took place in the beautiful Anglican Church, 'St. Mathews In The City'.

This then, was the beginning of a new family. Like so many of the children of early immigrants, they would eventually spread throughout New Zealand and in generations to come, across the world.

There was only the one love for Wilfred, and his wife Rose bore him five daughters, loving him in return until the day she left this life. There was one significant change Rose had made. From the time they met she called Wilfred by his second name 'Huia.' She said that he was her treasure and that the meaning of his name was perfect and so she always called him Huia.

Wilfred, now known as Bill by his many friends, was a spritely eighty, and had been a widower for four years. One day he received an unexpected visit from a very pleasant lady; a member of the Northcote Senior Citizens group of which he was President. He made her welcome, though was rather taken back when, over a cup of tea, she proposed that they married.

Her reasoning being that 'It was a shame two people rattled around in a house. Each alone and needing company – quite apart from the savings that could be made by them both,' and so on and so forth. Bill agreed that 'Yes, they did get along well together as friends but as far as …'

Afterwards he came to see me, to tell me what had happened. I asked "And how did you sort that out?"

"That was the easy part my dear. Told her the truth of course. That I had loved and will always love, only one woman. My wife Rose–your Mother–and this she accepted."

I put my arms around Dad and held him tight. This I had always known.

Just then the back door burst open and the children came rushing in, the youngest with cries of Poppa, Poppa." My eldest son, much more manly, quietly greeted his grandfather. Dad's eyes lit up; his favourite grandson, I knew. There had always been a special bond linking those two.

I listened to the children, all four talking at once, questions flying, answers slow to come. The next generation. Dad caught my eye and unspoken words passed between us.

We understand and smile.

*L to R: Aunt Rene Freeman, Rose Cave and Grandma May
Freeman. Taken at 24 Chamberlain St, Grey Lynn*

*Three sisters in front of 'the punishment sheds'.
Aunt Dorothy Christian, my mother Rose Cave and Aunt Rene*

My paternal grandfather Henry James Cave
in NZ Naval uniform

My maternal grandfather John Freeman, Capt of the NZ
steamship Taniwha. Taken on the Paeroa-Auckland run with
the Hauraki plains in the background.

THE GREAT ADVENTURE

Please take my hand and come with me, I would love your company on a walk down memory lane.

A lot of what I now write is from memory; sights, sounds and smells included. The rest is from what I was told by family during my growing years.

In 1936 my parents and elder sisters left farming on Great Barrier Island and returned to Auckland to live. The three eldest children were now in need of a college education, unavailable on the Barrier, and my mother had never adapted to the hardships of life on the Island. She was born and bred a city girl and more than happy to return to the Mainland!

I was born in Auckland two years later, my arrival being one of those unplanned events that happened to women in those days. My siblings, all sisters, were now fourteen, thirteen, twelve and six years of age. My father was now a milk vendor for Stonex Bros, collecting his deliveries from their processing plant at Newton. The effect of the 1930's depression had left its mark and anyone who had a job considered themselves fortunate. In later years I recall my father saying that in a sad way the outbreak of World War II, in 1939, was a blessing for the country. Full employment again!

At this time we lived in Takapuna. Mum was not at all happy when Father, without even consulting her, volunteered for duty in the NZ Army. When World War I was in progress he had, as a very young lad, travelled to

England and enlisted in the English Army where as a radio operator, he was placed in Signals for the duration of that war.

Now he was readily accepted by the NZ Army, and for mother to have family support nearby, a Housing Corp house in Grey Lynn was allocated, and here we would remain until the end of the war.

The ruling of the day for serving in the forces, was that single men went first, then married, then married with one child and so on. My father, having five children, was kept in New Zealand where his knowledge of long-range radio was put to good use. At the beginning, while up-skilling in long-range radio and Morse code, he also trained new recruits. For this reason he was initially based in Auckland at Sylvia Park Army Camp. It wasn't long before the New Zealanders were joined by American troops.

Their arrival here reinforced the saying by New Zealand men, particularly those in the forces, 'Overpaid, over-sexed and over here.' Jealousy? Quite likely.

Dad soon became part of a very active Signals Corp and eventually formed the Thames division which was based in Paeroa. We had therefore, a father who we still saw on a reasonably regular basis.

It is now the year nineteen-forty-two and I am almost four years old. It would appear that though I looked angelic, that was rather misleading, according to my sisters; of course.

On one particular day I couldn't get the attention of anyone. I had tried, and became tired of being shooed away. No one had time for me. "Go and play," they all said. Everyone busy, too busy for me. I sat on the front porch and sulked. I could smell the blossoms on the lemon tree that grew in the middle of the front lawn, and hear the bees buzzing away. Then I had a great idea and cheered up. There was one place where I could get all the attention I wanted. At Grandma's house.

Grandma was a widow and lived in a villa at 24 Chamberlain Street, off Richmond Road in Grey Lynn. I had never known my 'Grandpa Johnny' as my older sisters referred to him. Sadly, he died before I was born.

However, my lovely Aunt Rene, a spinster, still lived with Grandma. A warm-hearted lady who could always be depended on for times of fun. She reminded me of a little brown bird, as she dressed mostly in brown and cream, and flitted like a fantail from task to task, never still for long.

Grandma always made me welcome and would spend time with me in her garden, but she had very high expectations of children and I knew always to be on my best behaviour.

To get to Grandma's took a long, long time. A lot of walking for little legs. Of course I didn't stop to think of that, and decided to visit them.

I knew what I had to wear. I had two lots of 'going out' clothes as Mum called them. One for summer and one for winter. This day was lovely and warm so I dressed in my summer best. Then my frill-edged white socks and shiny black patent shoes and of course, my purse. A hankie was still in there, good. Now to rob my piggy bank as there was a store at the top of Grandma's street which sold yummy sweets. I was in luck, there were two pennies which went into my purse. As an afterthought I took my white sunhat and plonked it on my head. There, all ready.

I didn't bother to say goodbye to anyone. They were all too busy for me. And so I set out on my great adventure.

Once on the footpath I remembered to cross over to the other side of the road. This was to avoid the big loud dog that lived further along from our house. His bark hurt my ears and when he lunged and shook the fence, his hairy head seemed all teeth. He terrified me. I liked dogs, but not that one.

"Good morning young lady". The croaky voice came from behind the fence and the old man who Mum always stopped and chatted to, appeared. His back was very bent and from beneath scraggy eyebrows he looked down at me quizzically, asking, "And where are you going all on your own child? Where's your mum?"

"She's very busy, so I can go and visit Grandma and my aunt. And I've got money for sweets too." I took out the pennies from my purse and showed them to him.

With that he seemed satisfied and saying a polite goodbye, I went on my way.

The road led to what appeared to be a dead end, but wasn't. Well it was for cars, but not for people. A narrow concrete walking track sloped upwards to connect with the main road. This was Richmond Road which ran for miles and miles, circling the area.

As I walked up the track I passed the high wall of the Marist Brothers' monastery. The tall trees that grew on the other side of the brick walls hung out over the track and hid all the sun. Here it was dark and cold and I thought, spooky. I hurried to get out into the sunlight. Mum had explained about the walled grounds. Behind those walls was a home for men to be trained to be like ministers, and they remained behind those walls most of the time. I didn't like the sound of that and felt very sorry for them.

Coming out onto Richmond Road I walked on slowly up the steep street. The hot sun made my eyes squint and I began to wish I could have a drink of water. I looked all around me. The houses here were so very different from where I lived. Apart from only one or two that seemed to be made of white concrete or shiny bricks, they were wooden with high peaked rooves; older houses like Grandma's.

Most had verandas, and pretty front doors with coloured glass windows in them that glittered in the sun. Some of the houses looked like faces. The door was the mouth and the shining windows, one each side, being the eyes.

I stopped to watch bees buzzing all over two big shiny leaved bushes covered in pink blooms. There was one each side of the bricked walkway that led to the front steps. The same sort of bush was in lots of the small front gardens. I liked gardens, especially my grandma's.

I was very careful crossing the many side streets. 'Look right, look left and then look right again,' I remembered Mum saying. It was getting really noisy as the road levelled out and there were cars tooting and small trucks loaded with all sorts of goods. They roared along and at times let out blasts of pongy black smoke. Not very nice when you are only small and it was right in your face.

The trams joined in with their own special sounds. They swayed and rattled as they flew along the tram tracks, with the sound of clanging which they used as a warning. To me they said, 'watch out I'm here'. I loved the trams and riding in them was a wonderful treat. They didn't have a steering wheel, just a funny sort of metal handle. Even the shiny wooden seats had backs that moved so you could sit and face the other way. Great fun! The ticket collector in his smart uniform, and the cheerful driver with always a "Thank you Ma'am, Miss" as you left the tram. Then the warning ding, ding as they took off again.

I stopped to chat with a nice looking lady who was in her front garden picking roses. When I told her I was going to see my grandma she gave me two beautiful roses to take her saying, "Watch out for thorns, and hold them head down dear. I hope she likes them." I was very pleased, and thanked her before continuing on my way.

There were lots of cats on my walk. Cats of all colours and types. Some sleek and some fluffy. Some ran away but most were friendly. I would stop to pat them and listen to them purr. We didn't have a cat, though I would love to have one. Grandma didn't have a cat either. She loved to garden and said cat's droppings would not be appreciated!

I had reached the big school that my sister Irene who was ten, went to. I would go here too, when I was five. The school was painted a rich creamy colour and the windows were made up of dozens of small panes edged a deep reddish brown to match the double-doors and high peaked roofline. The school was close to the road and there was no grass, no trees. Just lots of tar seal where the children could play. This day the grounds were empty and quiet as school was closed for the weekend.

My legs were starting to get a wee bit tired and I was glad to follow a curve which led to where I would need to cross the main road. I hadn't thought about this when I set out. Now I found it a little scary. The traffic seemed to be coming from all directions, the noise deafening as I reached the gutter to cross over. I even felt the wind caused by the vehicles and then got some grit in my eyes. I took my hankie from my purse and stopped to wipe them.

There seemed to be a pause in the traffic so another glance both ways and I stepped out. I was part way across when a man in a big car shouted at me. "Get off the road girl." I shook as I tried to do just that. A tram was coming and I held my breath as I waited for it to pass. Now. I dashed across the tram tracks and was back on a footpath – phew, made it!

My feet were feeling really sore. Nearly there though. A little further on, just before the corner of Grandma's street, was the store. I thought of the pennies in my purse, opened the door and went in. The doorbell tinkled a welcome and I breathed in the lovely smells. In baskets sat loaves of bread, buns and biscuits freshly made. On one half of the long wooden counter was the most beautiful sight. Jar after jar of different lollies. Bullseyes striped in pink, Aniseed Balls a shiny brown, black Liquorice Straps, Marshmallows in pink and white. Brightly coloured boiled lollies, Coconut Ice, Fudge, Toffee Chunks, and fizzy tasting Sherbets, so many to choose from. Lovely.

"Hello dear," said the big lady that came through from the back of the shop. She straightened her pretty pinny and smiling down at me asked, "And how can I help you lass, are you all on your own today?"

Again I had to explain that I was on my way to Grandma's and that I had two pennies to spend. I put the roses down and taking the coins from my purse proudly showed her my money.

She nodded her head and held a paper bag, waiting for my choices. It was rather a lot of sweets for a little girl and I was very happy. Saying thank you, I picked up the rather floppy roses and left for the last of my walk.

Down Chamberlain Street I went. This was a steep street, or so it seemed to me. Almost there. I couldn't wait to taste the cold home-made ginger beer Aunt Rene would be sure to give me. I was very hot and very, very thirsty. I sucked on an Aniseed ball as I went – yum, and at last, there was number 24. The front door was open but I knew to go to the back door where I would remove my shoes and leave them in the closed-in porch.

Grandma didn't have a car – even the idea of Grandma driving made me giggle, but there was a tar-sealed drive along the side of the house towards an old unused garage.

I stepped into the cool of the porch, carefully closing the mesh door behind me and removed my hat and my shoes. Just as I had seen my mother do many times, I knocked on the door-frame and called, "Anyone home"?

Grandma was the first to arrive with Aunt Rene close behind. "Have you raced your mother here child?" Grandma asked.

Aunt added, "Look at the poor girl. She's all flushed with heat. Let her catch her breath Mother; a cold drink, that's what she needs." She drew me into the kitchen, sat me on a chair and hurried off to the pantry.

I told Grandma, "Mum isn't with me. I've come by myself." Grandma gave a gasp of horror!

Aunt Rene came back carrying a big shiny brown crock, and poured me a glass of her deliciously cold ginger beer.

Grandma told Aunt what I had done. Well, what a fuss. They both spoke at once and eventually it was decided that Aunt would go and tell my mother where I was. I would stay at Grandma's and they would walk me home tomorrow. This made me very happy.

Grandma did however, give me a sharp talking-to. She may have been a little woman but she had a strong, and at this moment, very stern voice. At the end of her finger-wagging lecture, I sobbed and promised never, ever, to go off on my own again. My tears soon dried as I watched Grandma take bread from the wood fired stove with the promise of some to eat when it had cooled.

I do not recall getting a hiding for 'going off' on my own, but this only happened the once – or so I was told. I'm sure if my father had been home at the time I would have been punished, as he firmly believed in the proverb 'Spare the rod and spoil the child.' Perhaps the good growling at from Grandma, combined with the frightening cars, trams and trucks I'd had to contend with, was enough to stop my wandering ever again.

And as I was taught always to be polite, thank you so much for your company on my walk down memory lane. I do hope you enjoyed it as much as I did.

My Grandma Freeman by the apple tree in her beloved garden

My parents, Rose and Wilfred (Bill) Cave, circa 1942

DIFFERENT TIMES

How very different childhood in the 1940's was to that of children today. In some ways we had more freedom, yet in others, were regimented in what we were allowed to do and say, and what we could not. This was a fine line from which I tumbled on many occasions.

It was quite normal for me, at the tender age of nine or ten, to go with a girlfriend to the beach, no adult supervision being deemed necessary. As long as we wore a hat and took a towel that was okay. If we were lucky, there would be a bottle of orange cordial to take with us. Mum made this sickly drink in a big pot, mixing heaps and heaps of sugar and water then adding the vivid orange cordial flavouring. No worries about the harm sugar caused back then!

Living at Northcote there were two swimming beaches from which to choose. Halls Beach near to the cinema, the best swimming beach, and Sulphur Beach near Stafford Park. The latter was rather shallow, and tide-dependant. We would spend hours at the beach, cooling off in the sparkling sea and scrambling over rocks and up cliffs with a total lack of fear; just having fun.

There were great times going 'mushrooming' with my older sisters. I cannot recall any rules about what land you could go on. I would be woken very early in the morning and after a quick breakfast we simply went walking. Being autumn, the mornings were always chilly, so we walked briskly. My sisters chatted non-stop, mostly boy talk and fashion. Boring to me so I usually raced ahead. When we saw a paddock with wee white spots dotted here and there, over the fence we would go; pouncing one by one on the round, newly-formed mushrooms that peered out from the moist grass. The best time for mushrooms apparently, was after a bit of rain. The billy cans were soon filled and we would troop home knowing that Mum and Dad would be pleased with our offerings.

One morning however, the unexpected happened. We were all heads down picking the delicacies when a voice shouted, "Hey, what do you think you're doing. Who said you could come on my land. You little beggars. Thieves, that's what you are, thieves, the lot of you."

I straightened up to see a big heavily bearded man in a red Swanndri jacket, with a woolly hat pulled down low on his ears. Wearing heavy boots he zig-zagged rapidly down the hill towards us.

"He's got a gun." I yelled.

Dolly said, "Time to go girls."

Irene nodded in agreement.

But Phena said, "Tip out the mushies and jump on them. Don't let him get them after all our hard work."

And she did exactly that. We all joined in, jumping up and down squashing the mushrooms underfoot. Laughing as we did so, until a deafening boom frightened the life out of us!

The farmer had fired a shot at us – or so we thought. Probably he'd fired over our heads to scare us and scare us he certainly did.

We ran like rabbits to, and up and over the fence; me falling down as I landed on the other side. Then ran like race horses until we were well out of the farmer's sight, finally stopping for breath. When we arrived home with empty billies and Mum heard why, we all laughed until our sides hurt. Shame about the mushrooms being wasted though. No mushrooms and bacon on toast that day.

Mum was an excellent and innovative cook. I guess all women were in those days. Usually there was only one wage earner in the family; the man of the house, so food had to be stretched as far as possible to feed the larger families of the time. Anything for free was welcome and blackberry picking came into this category. It was also a fun and productive pastime. With blackberries growing on the roadsides, at least there was no chance of being shot at! No poisonous spraying done then, either by councils or farmers, so blackberries were safe to pick. On farms, blackberry, like gorse, was grubbed out. Hard work, but effective.

Going home with full buckets or billies, we must have looked a sight. Purple stained fingers with mouths and chins to match, having eaten almost as many berries as we picked. The blackberry and apple pies Mum made were well worth our braving the prickles.

About this time I was regularly sent on an errand to the local chemist, a Mr. Rushton. Away I would go on my scooter, a bag with Mum's note in it dangling from one of the handle-bars. In the bag, Mum always placed a sealed envelope. I guess it contained a note and money. I would hand this to the chemist and he would retire to the back room saying "I won't be long young lady." I rather liked being called 'young lady' and deemed him ever so polite.

He would return with a square brown paper parcel in hand, and put this in the bag saying, "And a docket for your mother." I once asked Mum what was in the parcel. She told me, "Never you mind, my girl. It's not for you to know." In time I came to realise that I had been buying my sister's sanitary requirements for her 'monthlies.' How embarrassing! I avoided seeing Mr. Rushton for a long time after that.

Going to the movies was a real treat. The picture theatre was a mere ten minutes' walk from home. Recently the theatre had been upgraded from a cold hall-like, level floored building with hard seats, to a proper theatre. It now had sloping carpeted floors, soft leather seats and heating. Both of my parents enjoyed musicals which I loved, though Dad also enjoyed a good western.

Interval saw us in the lobby, my folks chatting with people they knew. I didn't like the cigarette smoke that the men puffed out fogging up the room, but the ice-creams were good. My favourite was the new Choc-Bombs, as Tip Top named them. Squat-shaped cones and flat-topped vanilla ice-cream coated in chocolate – super!

I was however, often embarrassed by my mother. When going out, ladies wore hats as well as gloves in those days, and the fashion in hats at the time was rather flamboyant. Decorations on often wide-brimmed hats included colourful flowers and feathers, wee birds, bright false fruit and berries. My Mum loved fashion and would re-style her hats to update them, being quite proud of her efforts.

At the movies however, these hats did cause a problem. I recall the time when a male voice from behind said, "Lady, how about removing that hat. I can't see a blooming thing."

Mum took no notice, continuing to stare straight ahead. The man then tapped her on the shoulder and in a louder voice, repeated his request. My mother turned and looking at him said in her most regal manner, "Young man, you are quite able to move I am sure. There are, after all, plenty of other seats available." The man and his companion did indeed move nearer to the front of the cinema. Father, I noticed, acted oblivious to the whole affair.

When talking with friends these days, the comment is often made on how particular things, for some odd reason, stay forever in your mind. A trip to visit Mother's cousins in Ponsonby was one such time. After a fun ferry trip across to Auckland we caught a tram from downtown Auckland to Three Lamps, Ponsonby. The tram rattled along swaying gently from side to side, and all too soon the ride was over.

A short walk down from the main road took us to a house which was high up in the air – or so it seemed to me-as there were a lot of steps going up to the front door. At each side of the steps big clumps of strong-smelling white lilies were almost overpowering. Arum lilies, Mum told me.

These two ladies whom I called Aunt, were probably much older than my parents. Isabel and Alice made us welcome and we sat in their parlour for a while. I know I was fidgeting because my mother quietly told me to sit up straight and, sit still.

"Before we have lunch," Aunt Isobel began, "perhaps you would like to go and see Father." I followed everyone into a bedroom where a big man lay prone on a very large bed. "This is your Great Uncle Walter," Aunt

Alice told me, and she took me to the side of the bed. He held out a pudgy hand saying "Hello child."

I didn't like the look of him. His face was blotchy, his nose red with blue veins tracing the surface, and his watery eyes were heavy-lidded. Lizard-like. But he smiled, so I took his hand.

Aunt Isobel asked, "Do you know how old your Uncle is, dear?

"No Aunt," I quietly replied.

"Well," she said proudly, "He is almost one hundred years old!"

I thought about that for a minute or two then asked the old man, "Why aren't you dead then?"

There was absolute silence.

Then the old man coughed, spluttered and wheezed, his hands grasping at the coverlet. My aunts fussed and my parents quickly took me from the room back to the parlour, where a lecture on good manners began. What a terrible thing to have said to the poor old man. The lecture went on and on. When would I remember to think before I spoke?

No wonder this visit remained forever in my mind!

Childhood years passed quickly and by the time I left college and obtained my first job there were only two of us girls still living at home.

My first job after leaving college was as a sales assistant in a shoe shop. During the year I had been there I learned a lot. First rule of serving customers–the customer is always right! In those days you served your customers. They sat in a comfortable chair, the sales person sitting on the high end of a low stool. On the sloping end of the stool you measured the customer's foot using a metal sliding device to check the correct shoe size required. Then having ascertained the style of shoe needed and the preferred colour, you began to bring down one box of shoes after another, fitting them onto the customer's feet until she/he was satisfied. Twenty or more pairs of shoes were often left to be put away, even when no sale was made.

I particularly enjoyed serving children. There was a machine which showed in X-ray form the shape of the child's foot within a shoe. Very important for allowing for growth, and using this machine always fascinated the children as well as impressing the parents.

One day as I walked down Queen Street heading for the Ferry buildings and home, I saw in a bookshop window, an advertisement for a shop assistant. The shop, I noted, also sold magazines and newspapers, and being close to the Ferry buildings, it seemed to be very busy.

From behind the counter a sandy haired young woman saw me reading the advertisement and smiled at me. I went in and when she was free from serving customers, asked her about the job. The manager was out, he'd just gone to the bank. She had been working there nearly two years and really enjoyed her job. I took an instant liking to her and thought she had a lovely warm smile so I decided to wait to talk to the manager. Little did I know then, that Joyce, who I had just met, was to become a very special life-long friend!

After a meeting with the manager I was hired to start in two weeks, as I needed to give notice to my existing employer. This new job was to prove a real eye opener!

Only a few days after I began work, Joyce took me to one side and murmured that there was something I should know about the manager. She was rather red-faced, and I soon understood why. She explained that there had been a run of young ladies who had not stayed long in the job. Why? I wanted to know. It seemed the manager had offended them by making 'passes' at them in his little office out the back.

I asked Joyce "Well, why have you stayed here so long. Hasn't he made passes at you?"

"Oh no," she said. "I am, as you may have noticed, short and a bit on the plump side. It seems he only likes tall slim girls."

"Well, he better not try anything on with me," I told her. "I won't put up with anything like that!"

Nothing happened and after a few weeks I forgot all about Joyce's warning. One day we had just got over the lunchtime rush when I heard my name called. "In here please, I need you for a minute." Into the cupboard-like office I went. "I've gone and got ink on my trousers," the boss said. "Here, there's ink remover on this cloth, if you'd just clean my trousers for me."

I looked down at where he indicated and noted just where the area of ink was. "You dirty old man," I shouted. "You can stick your job." I grabbed my cardigan and handbag and hurried through the shop. Ignoring the looks from the couple of customers browsing, I told Joyce, "You were right, and I'm not staying in this blooming job. I'll give you a ring tonight."

Jobs were plentiful then. As long as you dressed tidily, spoke well, could add up, and were polite, there were plenty of jobs to choose from. In actual fact, that

218

grubby manager had done me a favour, as after that I was employed in my first clerical position. No more tired and aching legs by the end of the working day, no late night to work and, better pay as well!

Over the ensuing years Joyce and I often laughed heartily recalling that event. Interesting though that I never told my parents why I'd left the bookshop. I couldn't possibly talk to them about that sort of thing. Anyway, they were just happy that I had a better job.

I often wondered if that creepy manager finally got his just desserts. I certainly hope so.

Margaret Cave, 16, and Joyce Heyes at 18, in Auckland city

About the Author

Born in Auckland, New Zealand, Margaret Hunter is a retired business woman. She lives with her husband Rod, and recently-adopted cat Smooch, in the delightful Waikato town of Te Aroha.

She is the proud matriarch of three generations and draws on many of life's experiences in her writings.

Made in the USA
Columbia, SC
13 May 2017